SPIKE AND FRIENDS

SPIKE AND FRIENDS

George A.M. Heroux

Strategic Book Publishing and Rights Co.

Strategic Book Publishing & Rights Co., LLC
USA | Singapore
www.sbpra.net

For information about special discounts for bulk purchases, please contact Strategic Book Publishing and Rights Co. Special Sales, at bookorder@sbpra.net.

ISBN: 978-1-68235-297-7

TABLE OF CONTENTS

ACKNOWLEDGEMENTS

Spike and friends is a book of fiction riddled with true stories of three life-long friends, Bud Twiss, Earl Quantock, and this author. Bud was, indeed, a fine lawyer but a very mischievous young man. He did graduate second in his law school class and had a brilliant career. Earl Quantock was military all the way, served in Vietnam, was tragically injured in battle, and became a very fine high school teacher after he could no longer serve. Many of the other stories come from my own career as a lawyer and victim advocate. While I have taken great liberty with the facts, making this book a novel rather than a biography/ autobiography, much of what you will read is mere reporting of what happened, regardless of how incredible the stories may seem. Even close friends and family will not identify any of us specifically as one of the characters; I have freely distributed credit and blame as I saw fit.

I want to acknowledge the wonderful assistance and inspiration received from my three daughters, Marcia Heroux Pounds, Karen Turner, and Marijean Oldham. All three were instrumental in ensuring that the writing was clear, concise, and accurate. Their mother, Jean, has always provided encouragement and advice in everything I have ever written.

SPIKE AT 32

The publicity that our firm received from the Harry Jackson murder trial made us a remarkably successful firm over the next year. The decision as to whether to concentrate our practice in the criminal or in the civil area was made for us. Suddenly, we were being retained by criminals with money. Let me put it another way: We were hired to defend individuals who were charged with major crimes who had the money to pay us. Tony and I preferred to defend the innocent defendant, but we also felt that even a criminal deserves Constitutional rights. Even the worst criminal, we thought, had the right to the best legal representation possible. That was us, we figured. We lost some, but won many more cases than we lost. We defended people accused of embezzlement, grand larceny, manslaughter, murder – all the good stuff. We were so successful that we were able to add several members to the firm, Tony was able to get home for dinner on time – except when we were in the middle of a trial – and Ellen and I took a 10-day cruise. Life was good.

There were some strange cases and odd defendants along the way, though. One was Charlotte Wilson and her reckless homicide charge. She was being held in the county jail when her husband visited with us at the office. I disliked him immediately, but he had the necessary retainer fee that convinced us to talk to him. He was a big guy with a protruding jaw and a brash, cocky personality. If he had told me his name was Joe Slick, I would have believed him.

"I should be charged, not her," Brad Wilson said. "They haven't charged me with anything, but I'm kind of guilty, too. We were both drunk. That's how it all started."

"All right, Brad," Tony said, "we know that your wife has been charged with reckless homicide in the death of a forty-two-year woman. Let's take it from the beginning."

"Yeah, sure. I guess the beginning was when Charlotte and I were invited to her boss's home for his birthday. It was a big to-do at his hotshot home by the lake. I guess there were eighty, ninety people there. The eats were plentiful and so was the booze. Let's say that we were both enjoying the free alcohol, but Charlotte was leaving me in her dust. The more she drank, the more she flirted with every guy there. Finally, I had enough. I told her that I was getting the hell out of there."

"You left her at the party?" Tony asked.

"Yeah. Her boss picked up on what was going on. He's not a bad guy. He told me that he would make sure she got home all right. He'd have one of his non-drinking employees take her home."

"Didn't that happen?" Tony asked.

"It did happen, I guess, but she didn't come into the house when she got there. She took off again in her car. I don't know what got into her to take off like that. That's when she hit Mrs. Denton. The police said that she was driving at a high rate of speed, went over to the other side of the road, and hit the woman head-on."

"All right. We'll talk to Charlotte in her cell," I said. "The drunk driving laws are tough. Most people end up pleading guilty because there's not much of a defense for killing someone by driving drunk, but for the time being, she's going to plead not guilty. Is there anything else you would like to tell us before we talk to Charlotte?"

"I don't know what she'll tell you. Maybe our stories won't be exactly the same. As I said, we were both drinking – a lot."

Later that afternoon, we were able to see Charlotte in the county jail. If I had run a dating service, I would have set her up with her husband. She was as brash and cocky as he was, just a great deal more attractive. Her orange jail garb didn't hide a bountiful body. Everything about her said "I want to have a good time," but now she was in serious trouble. Being convicted of reckless homicide by drunk driving was good for a three-to-fourteen-year prison sentence. After a brief introduction and after telling her that we had been hired by her husband, I opened the questioning.

"Our understanding is that you were driven home after an evening of drinking but instead of going into your home, you got into your car and sped onto a main two-lane road. Is that what happened?"

"No, not by a long shot. I may have been drunk, but I remember it all."

Wonderful, I thought, *already we're getting contradictory stories.*

'Okay," Tony said, "suppose you tell us what happened from the beginning."

"Yes, I did drink quite a bit at my boss's party and yes, I did get a ride home, but I did go into the house. That's when it got ugly."

"Ugly?" I said. "How?"

"Brad was really steamed when he left the party, so he wasn't home when I got there. He had gone to a bar where he hangs out with his dumbo friends sometimes."

"So, you didn't get into your car immediately," Tony said.

She smiled and shook her head. "No, I was calling it a night. I undressed and went to bed within minutes of getting home."

"All right," I said, "so tell me how you got from bed to your car. When did that happen?"

3

"Here's where the ugly comes in," she said. "When Brad got home, he woke me up. He started screaming about how he told his friends what a bitch I was and how he was going to beat the crap out of me when he got home. Then he started slapping me even before I could get out of bed."

"And?" Tony said.

"And I wasn't about to take it lying down. I was at him with my fists, my fingernails, my knee, everything I had. Sure, I was still drunk and so was he. We had a vicious brawl. He was slamming at me and I was tearing at him. I know I got into his mouth once and tore his lip. There was a lot of blood. That's when I got scared. Then, he started hitting me with his fists. I thought he was going to kill me. That's when I ran."

"Out of the house?" Tony asked.

"Right to my car. I always leave my keys on the dashboard and I don't lock the car. I jumped in and drove off as fast as I could."

"The crash was within minutes of your home. Do you remember it?" I asked.

"As I said, I remember it all. I wanted to get away from home as fast as I could. I was sure he was going to kill me if he caught me. Yeah, I remember the crash. I knew I was going fast and that I wasn't handling the car very well. I saw the car coming on the other side of the road, but I couldn't stop my car from going there somehow. It was awful. After the crash, I was trapped in the car, so I didn't know until later that I had killed somebody."

Then Tony asked a question that surprised me because I didn't think of it. "Charlotte, you fought with your husband directly from your bed. Did you leave the house so quickly that you were still wearing a night gown or pajamas?"

Charlotte gave us a moment so that she could intrigue us with her reply. "No, I was naked. I always sleep in the nude. That what I do."

I couldn't help but picture the scene of her running out the door completely naked, hopping in her car, and speeding off. I think that Tony had the same image.

"Of course," Charlotte continued, "when the police and emergency people arrived, they saw that I was not only traumatized by the crash and drunk but also quite naked."

* * *

Seldom is there any defense for driving drunk and killing someone, but after putting our heads together, Tony and I thought we might have one. In a drunk driving reckless homicide, we would customarily advise the defendant to plead guilty, hoping that the judge would take the guilty plea into consideration when determining the sentence. After all, it saves all that court time and the need to impanel a jury. Not this time. We went to trial with a possible defense.

Tony's opening statement set the stage for our unusual defense. "We believe that driving drunk and causing a death is a horrible crime," Tony told the jury. "But what if the drunk driver somehow has no choice but to be in this terrible position of being a drunk driver? That is what we're going to explain in testimony presented during this trial. You will understand our defense when you hear the only witness that we will be putting on the stand, Brad Wilson, the defendant's husband."

The prosecutor's case was solid and not difficult to prove. The State's Attorney, John Mills, presented testimony by a police officer who was the first to arrive at the scene, by an emergency rescue professional who told the jury how he excavated Charlotte from the car, of course mentioning her nudity, and by a hospital technician who tested her blood alcohol content. Except for some minor clarifications, there was little we could do on cross-examination.

Clearly, Charlotte was drunk, a .16 blood alcohol content, twice the legal limit of .08, and it was established that she was the driver who admitted her inability to remain on her side of the road and as a result was responsible for the death of Sheila Denton, a 42-year-old nurse returning from her late shift at the hospital.

Brad had given us some fascinating information between the first time he sat in our office and the time we were about to put him on the stand. First, he admitted the fight with his wife. He had conveniently left that out when we first talked to him. Then, he told us how he had raised bail for her and how they had "made up." Finally, he announced that she was pregnant. These facts compelled our use of him as a witness along with the simple fact that we needed him to establish the only possible defense.

I was a bit surprised to hear about how they had "made up." It had been quite an effort to get the judge to allow bail in a manslaughter case. I assumed that the couple were well on the way to divorce but, alas, no.

I cringed a bit when Brad winked at Charlotte as he took the stand. Worse, Charlotte, in full view of jury members, smiled and returned the wink. God, I thought, jury members are going to hate these people, but I just had to deal with that in my questioning.

"Mr. Wilson, you are married to the defendant, Charlotte Wilson," I began. "Is that correct?"

"Yes, sir," he responded, "We've been married for eight years."

"But not always happily, I understand. Is this correct?"

"We've had our good times and our bad times," he said. "My biggest problem with Charlotte was that she was such a flirt. Maybe she was what you might call outgoing, but it seemed to me that she was coming on to guys. As you see, she's a very beautiful woman." More smiles from our defendant.

"Please tell the jury about the party you and the defendant attended during the early evening of the night of the crash."

"That party really got to me. I took her flirting around because I thought maybe she did that because of her job, but I had enough. I left her there and went to have a few drinks with my friends. When I told them about it, they said I shouldn't let her get away with that stuff. The more we talked and the more I thought about it, the madder I got. Finally, I told them that I was going to go home and beat the, you know, out of her."

"And what happened when you arrived at your home?"

"She was sleeping, lying there in the nude like always. I woke her up with a slap across her face. I guess I hit her a few more times. I wanted to teach her a lesson."

"And how did she respond to these slaps?" I asked.

"She came at me like a screaming banshee. She's got those long nails, and she used them. Then, I was really mad. I started hitting her harder. She got me pretty good, too."

"Mr. Wilson," I said, "at that point, were you so angry that her life was in danger?"

"Absolutely. I went crazy. I think I might have killed her if she hadn't run out of the house."

"Did you chase after her?"

"Yeah, a few seconds later. My mouth was bleeding. She tore my lip somehow. I stopped to look in the mirror to see where all the blood was coming from. I didn't think she'd leave the house, her being naked and all."

"But you did pursue her?"

"Yeah, I was even madder, but by the time I got to the door, she was pulling away in her car."

"I want you to consider carefully your response to this question, Mr. Wilson. At that time, did you intend to kill your wife?"

"No question about it. If I had caught her, she'd be dead now."

Then Tony whispered something to Charlotte that was rash and crude but perhaps necessary. "If you don't stop smiling, I'm going to kill you myself." I think that she got the message.

I asked him the question again with some important rephrasing: "You are admitting to a crime, attempted murder. Taking that into consideration, do you still say that it was your intention to kill your wife?"

"I believe it was at that time."

On cross-examination, the erstwhile State's Attorney picked up on Wilson's friendliness with his wife in court.

"Have you and your wife now made up from your argument that night? Are you now back living together?"

"Yes, we are back together," Wilson said. "I visited her in the county jail every day and she moved back in with me when she got out on bail. We've worked out our differences."

"And now she is not afraid that you will kill her. Is that right?"

"No, no, that's all in the past. In fact, we don't drink anymore, and now she understands how I feel about that flirting thing."

State's Attorney Mills' closing argument consisted of restating the evidence that Charlotte was proven to be over the legal limit of alcohol when she crashed into Mrs. Denton, and then he argued that the couple's reconciliation belied the claim that Charlotte was truly fearful for her life when she sped off in the vehicle.

My closing argument was comprised of a single theory, the right of Charlotte to flee to save her life. This was justification under the law, I pointed out, to commit a crime if it was necessary; she was facing certain death if she did not get away as fast as she could even if it meant driving while intoxicated. The fact that she took an innocent life, I said, was a tragedy but was a consequence of avoiding certain death for herself.

The judge agreed to my requested instruction to the jury that flight to avoid death was a legitimate reason for violating the law. That was the clincher. It took the jury around ten hours to reach a decision, but they returned with a Not Guilty verdict on the reckless homicide. They did find her guilty of drunk driving. This was a strange verdict since they absolved her of the major crime because of a right to flee but found her guilty of the lesser crime even though the same logic existed to forgive her that crime. That left us with a sentencing on the DUI charge. I had to convince the judge, then, that she should not go to jail for that crime even though the drunk driving resulted in a death. For the sentencing, I did put her on the stand. I knew that she would demonstrate her sorrow for taking a life – and I knew that she would demonstrate her pregnancy by wearing maternity clothes. She was given twenty-six weeks of home imprisonment to be served before and after the delivery of the baby.

Back in the office, Tony and I discussed the case the day after the sentencing.

"Why don't we feel good about this win?" Tony asked.

"Maybe it's because justice isn't always accomplished when you win. That may have been the case this time."

"Well," Tony said, "I hope that the Denton family gets big bucks out of the Wilsons and their insurance company in a civil action."

"Could be. One thing I know for sure: We're not going to be involved in the civil defense. Actually, Tony, we may be coming to the end of our law practice together."

"What?" Tony said.

"Now that the State's Attorney has lost two high profile cases to us, I was contacted early this morning by the Democratic Party's leadership. They want me to run for State's Attorney. Want to be a First Assistant State's Attorney?"

TONY AT 10

Spike Dumbrowski's parents married a few months after his birth, a little less than a year after Chuck Dumbrowski poured a substantial amount of alcohol into the party punch bowl at a one-year high school reunion. Chuck's objective, of course, was to liven up the party and, in the process, become a hero to his classmates, all of whom preferred the spiked punch to the tamer variety. Spike's mother was shocked when she discovered that she was pregnant. I have no information as to whether there were other conceptions that night. Chuck was amused to the degree that he referred to the unborn child as Spike from the very beginning. Both Chuck and Betsy were not unhappy with the unexpected pregnancy. Getting married had been their goal for a long time; the arrival of Charles, Jr., a.k.a. Spike, simply accelerated plans. In the beginning of the marriage, Chuck was ecstatic with his accomplishment. He boasted to friends of his virility and of the strapping son, albeit a bit of a featherweight, who would no doubt be heavyweight champion of the world someday. Only later did Mr. Charles Dumbrowski become somewhat less satisfied with the arrangement; he felt overburdened with the responsibility of supporting and caring for a wife and child. This led to after-work hours and evenings with friends at the local saloon. Occasionally, he remembered he had a son, but, when he did, he struck upon an unusual way of demonstrating his love for his son: He took Spike to the bars with him. This happened mostly when Spike was five or six years old, an age when a boy could be quite interesting in an environment that included a group of drinking men. Spike told jokes, posed riddles, generally entertained, and befriended everyone in the establishment. Mostly, he just talked and talked, much to the amusement of the bar's patrons. Chuck didn't really settle in to the task of being a parent until Spike was ten years old. Then, he felt that being a good father was to be a good disciplinarian. It may have been too late. About that time, Spike began enjoying life but for the hanging.

One time that year, a trio of ruffians scared Spike half to death. They decided that he should be hanged for his crime of being friendly to a girlfriend of one of the boys; she thought he was "cute." They grabbed him on his way home late one night and put a rope around his neck and an A&P paper bag over his head as though they were going to string him up. Of course, they had no intention of doing that. They just wanted to scare the bejesus out of him. Catching him alone on his way home from school, they announced their criminal intentions. The existence of the rope made their promise all the more convincing. Spike attempted to dissuade them by announcing that he was meeting Curley McBride on that very street corner. Curley was bigger than any of the boys that he saw in front of him and probably twice as mean as any of them. This did give the ruffians some pause, but they then deduced that there was no way Curley would be seen with the likes of Spike. In the end, all they did was tack him on a tall telephone pole by looping him by the back of his belt on a pole step that was about six feet high. They hadn't tied his hands, so Spike was able to remove the bag and unbuckle the belt to gain access to the ground again, but it was an experience that was so intensely embarrassing that he never forgot it. Neither did the ruffians.

Spike was my friend. It was a long time before he related to me the terrible tale of his kidnapping and hanging. I was incensed to learn of this vile treatment of Spike. In my estimation, he was completely innocent of any misbehavior and certainly didn't deserve what had been done to him. On the spot, I vowed to help him seek revenge. I was a willing participant in carrying out any plan that would affect some measure of revenge. Therefore, we put our heads together. (As it turned out, in the process of our deliberations, we heard a strange noise coming from the basement level of the building directly alongside where we were standing. Simultaneously, we stooped to determine the cause of this disturbance only to bang our heads against each other, so we literally put our heads together that day.) After the dizziness subsided (and after I was able to smile at Spike's ill-timed comment that "that was getting two good heads together"), we were able to structure our plan for revenge.

There was more than one sin committed by these boys against Spike. One was putting much too much emphasis on the first vowel of his last name, pronouncing it DUMB- browski; sometimes DUMB-BREWski was the term they used. We found both nicknames to be offensive, of course, because Spike was neither dumb nor a consumer of beer. In later years, as you will see, the brew part of the nickname had some credence; the dumb was never appropriate.

The big boys at the time were fourteen or fifteen with not much hope of graduating from the eighth grade unless, of course, the desks were simply too small for them and it became necessary to move them on to an unsuspecting high school. At ten, breezing through the fifth grade, Spike and I foresaw no similar problems. In fact, that was a reason for their hate. Unconventionally, when there wasn't a pick-up baseball game going on, we found it quite normal to sit around the sewer drain and discuss the lessons learned in school any given day. Simply put, we were interested in what we learned at school while the big boys could hardly wait to expel the knowledge thrust at them during the school day in favor of more pernicious activity.

Spike was short for his age at the time. We didn't know that he would reach a time in high school when he would spring out of his shoes and clothes into a massively built, how's-the-weather-up-there kind of guy. For the fifth-grade time being, however, he was very conscious of his height. Being picked up and attached to a telephone pole by bigger boys exacerbated the problem. There may have been a few other reasons for the bigger boys' dislike of Spike. Certainly, he was eminently smarter than they were. That was not difficult. However, he had a manner of demonstrating his superiority in a way that was embarrassing to them. In a cool but dispatched way, he would correct them when they said or did something ignorant in his presence in the schoolyard. Told to "get lost, kid," he would shrug his shoulders with the clear message that he was clever and they were, well, just plain dumb. Nevertheless, surely this behavior of Spike's did not earn the hanging.

We had been buddies, Spike and I – Tony Boudreau – since we both managed to convince the nuns at St. Anne's that we were quite capable of jumping over kindergarten to the first grade. After that, it was a matter of which one of us could show up a nun by correcting her whenever there was a misinterpretation of a history, geography, or arithmetic fact. This was easy for the most part because, one, we pored over the assigned material while the nuns relied on their teaching preparations from prior year semesters and, two, the nuns were of a French-Canadian order and had a few language interpretation problems occasionally. I have no idea of the extent of the nuns' formal education. After all, they had to learn how to be nuns first and teachers second.

It may be that their education was not extensive. However, their habits alone demanded respect.

"Vengeance shall be mine," Spike quoted from a movie or something; he wasn't sure nor was I.

"Look," I said, "we can't pummel these guys as surely as they deserve to be beaten within an inch of their lives, so we have to hurt them in some other way."

That's when we began to develop our diabolical plan. "We need to embarrass them. They need to feel shame," Spike said.

"Anonymous phone calls to their mothers?" I ventured.

"No, no. That won't do it." Clearly that idea was not good enough – and certainly not creative enough. Besides, I think it is safe to say that their parents had grown accustomed to receiving negative comments about these particular sons from a variety of neighbors and teachers.

"How about we leave a note for Sister Agnes Marie – unsigned, of course - that reports that they have a venereal disease and should be sent home?"

"Not bad," Spike said, "except that we're not entirely sure what a venereal disease is."

"Well, it's something bad for sure," I retorted.

"We have to come up with something that won't be blamed on us. It has to be something that could have been hatched by anyone," Spike said. "Surely, there are a lot of kids that would like to get even with these guys for something they did."

That's when Spike hatched the plan that would reach fruition the following weekend. It all started with our knowing that there would be a middle-school basketball game on Friday night and that the ruffians would be playing. While the boys were out on the floor, Spike and I stealthily entered the boys' locker room. We had watched the arrival of the boys very carefully, noting the clothes that they were wearing. Since all the boys of St. Anne's

Catholic School trusted each other implicitly, making it totally unnecessary to use locks, we opened locker doors until we found the targeted clothes. We placed the clothing of the three boys, all of their clothing, in a large sack. Again, moving quietly, we lifted the bag of clothes and walked it to the doorstep of Sister Cook. We knew that her door was the entrance to the kitchen and that room would be empty long after the dinner hour, giving us ample time for a getaway. Obviously, Sister Cook was not the nun's name as we were reminded often by the other nuns who did the teaching while the aforementioned nun prepared the meals and kept the convent in order. I don't believe that we ever did know her name.

Spike banged on the door loudly as soon as we dropped the bag, and we were off and running. Imagine the bewilderment of the nuns to receive this unwanted gift along with the puzzle of what on earth to do with it.

Years later, one of the boys forgivingly told me what happened. After the game's final buzzer, our victims were shocked to view their empty lockers. Worse, they had to face a predicament: Should they meet their parents in the parking lot in twenty-two-degree weather with no satisfactory answer to why they had not showered and changed or should they go on a search around the school for the missing clothes? Of course, the clothes could be anywhere. Surely, this was not a total theft but a temporary relocation of the clothes, they reasoned. Clearly, it was a mischievous or villainess stunt, and the clothes had to be somewhere nearby. At first, they ran the corridors and peeked into classrooms and closets. Then they saw the note that we had tacked to the outside door. It said: Your clothes are outside. Then – horrors – they were compelled to step outside into the cold weather to expand their search. Obviously, they were surprised when they darted around the school in the cold to see two nuns holding a large bag.

"Is this what you're looking for?" asked one of the nuns.

"I … we … our …" stuttered one of the ruffians.

"Apparently so," Sister Rose said. "Mother Superior will want an explanation the first thing Monday morning in her office," Sister said.

All that the boys could do was grab the bag of clothes and run back to the gym before suffering any further frigid air and humiliation.

Spike's father was a cantankerous son of a gun. Although he had a full-time job, he spent many evenings as a part-time mechanic in his extra garage working on neighbors' cars. Much of our education in profane words came from hearing Chuck Dumbrowski as he struggled with a stubborn bolt or an errant gasket. Often, we were within hearing range as we tossed a basketball at the driveway hoop. Actually, we didn't need to be that close; one could hear his exasperated outbursts for a distance. He once told us that he "enjoyed" working on cars. That statement puzzled us no end because his behavior while he was at it appeared to us to be the exact opposite of enjoyment. Nevertheless, that activity, along with his full-time job, must have satisfied his inclination to avoid a great deal of parenting.

Chuck Dumbrowski ignored his son except for those times when he felt it necessary to insure Spike's manliness. One of those times was when Spike got into a scuffle one evening outside of Duncan's grocery store with a sixth grader also of the ruffian variety. The fight was broken up by other boys hanging around that particular corner but not before Spike suffered a shiner. Mr. Dumbrowski took his mind off the '42 Chevy long enough to demand a description in detail of the event that caused Spike's sorrowful-looking eye. When Spike truthfully reported that the other kid was pretty much undamaged, his father told him not to come home to dinner until and unless he successfully decorated

Spike's opponent with a similar bruise. Spike missed dinner that night, huddling in the cold. I can't say for certain what was going through Spike's mind, but I know that he had no particular interest in taking on the bigger boy for the second time in a day; yet, he had to take some action to gain readmission to his house. Eventually, hoping to return to a warm bed if not dinner, he found the courage to ring a doorbell and – in full view of the young man's family at the front door – dispensed a semi-vicious blow. Mission accomplished, he turned and ran for his life. The receiver of the blow stayed away from Spike after that, not because he was afraid of him but because he admired his audacity and thought that he might be capable of worse bold atrocities.

"Are you serious?" I asked. "His parents were standing right there when you hit him?"

"You bet," Spike said, clearly proud of his courage brought about by a fear of his unreasonable father. I, of course, admired not only his singular courage but his well thought out plan that resulted in accomplishing his mission while avoiding any chance of blows being returned thanks to his fleet feet and the selection of the war zone.

One of our favorite activities during the winter months of Upstate New York was to stand about a dozen feet alongside the road and pepper passing motorists with snowballs. If the motorist stopped, we had our escape plan designed to hide away in Mr. Denault's cellar in the dark, alongside of his stacks of beer cases. We always wondered if he drank the beer directly from the cellar or whether the beer bottles were cooled in the kitchen fridge on the way to Mr. Denault's taste buds. When the motorist did not stop but would speed up to get away from our snowballs, we had a surprise. Although our snowballs were of a normal size when thrown from the side of the road, Spike always prepared smaller ones that he could throw a long, long way. Just when the motorist thought he was out or range, one of Spike's mini snowballs would come out of the sky for another direct hit. It never occurred to any of us that this would be a dangerous distraction for the driver, but we did avoid throwing at women drivers in our sexist, young decision-making.

Since television and video games were only in the future for us at the time, mischief was our primary form of entertainment. Oh, sure, my parents didn't approve of some of these activities, but because I had ten brothers and sisters (more about this later), there was hardly time to keep tabs on my whereabouts or to reign me in. One popular sport was the mostly harmless activity of ringing doorbells and running away. This would not have been all that entertaining for us except that Mr. Benoit would bolt out the door and chase us for a block or two. In retrospect, I'm sure that it was never his intention to catch us. However, chasing was sport for him and a semi-terror for us. Just once, he caught one of us, quite by accident. Our other good buddy, Frank Foley, an 11-year-old who often joined in on this activity, had already developed a smoking habit. As he ran from a pursuer, you could see the cigarette glow in the dark as he carried it with him. Mr. Benoit was also a smoker. One time, Spike darted behind a garage and sat behind a bush, reasoning that he had run far enough. Not looking closely enough, he revealed himself to a smoking figure only to discover that it was not Frank, our smoking colleague, but Mr. Benoit who also carried a lit cigarette. The sudden meeting was embarrassing for both Spike and Mr. Benoit.

"Hi," Spike said, completely lost as to what else to say.

"I'm taking you to the police," Mr. Benoit said, also at a loss as to how he should handle the situation if he actually caught one of the mischief makers.

"What did I do?" feigned the astonished Spike.

Mr. Benoit rallied. "I'm going to let you go this time. No more ringing my doorbell. You understand?"

"Scout's honor," Spike said, as he darted away.

Paradoxically, some thirty years later, a ten-year-old in my neighborhood began ringing and running. It amused me that he and his friends reminded me of our activity at that age. Somewhat in honor of Mr. Benoit, I ran out the door one evening in pursuit of the boys only to give them the thrill we experienced as kids. To my horror, I was suddenly within grabbing distance of my next-door neighbor's child. He dropped to one knee and said "I didn't do it, I didn't do it." "It's okay," I said, "I used to ring doorbells when I was your age." I was really embarrassed that I frightened the kid. I went out of my way to be friendly with him whenever I saw him after that. That turned out to be wise. Thirty years later, he was my sports injury doctor who occasionally injected me with a humongous needle for problems such as arthritis and trigger fingers. I never reminded him of the time I nabbed him for ringing my doorbell.

After Mr. Benoit "caught" Spike, we decided that he was too nice a guy to bother any more. We moved on to a grouch who desperately wanted to grab us in the act of committing one of our petty crimes. This spiced up the danger and consequently the adventure. And so it was that we determined that bell ringing was an insufficient nuisance for this man, Mr. Forgette. That's when Spike hatched yet another monster plan.

One of my older acquaintances worked at the newly opened A&P. We asked him to leave a number of assorted boxes at the top of the A&P dumpster. Spike's plan was to drop some of the boxes on Mr. Forgette's front porch immediately after ringing the doorbell. Then, we reasoned, Mr. Forgette would run out of the door and tumble into the boxes, creating some bedlam. It worked to perfection. He kicked, stumbled, and fell onto some of the boxes as expletives roared from his mouth.

Since we were a full two blocks from Mr. Denault's beer cellar, we had a different plan altogether for this event. Right across from Mr. Forgette's house was a vacant lot. At the far side, there was a rather high wooden fence that lead into a neighbor's yard. During the day leading up to our attack on Mr. Forgette's premises, we practiced jumping the fence. A bit on the long-legged side, I was particularly adept at this. I could hurtle the fence on the run. Spike had to stop and scramble over the fence; nevertheless, he could also reach safe ground on the other side, albeit with a bit more effort. After the initial foray, Spike thought that a second attack would be a marvelous thing. After all, we still had a supply of boxes.

"Come on," Spike urged us. "Let's do it. This guy is going to have a conniption." We weren't sure what a conniption was, but we were sure it was the right word.

"I think that we should get one guy to go, ring the bell, drop a few boxes, and get out of there," Frank suggested. "Who wants to go?"

"Let's throw for it," Frank suggested. This premise consisted of two boys flipping their hands out with an undetermined number of fingers pointed outward as one of the participants hollered odds or evens. If the combined fingers that were held out added up to the odd or even that was called, the caller won. If not, the other finger-thrower won, of course. Frank's organization of this competition was less than perfect. Instead of a structured round-robin or elimination tournament to find an ultimate winner, Frank suggested that he take on everyone until he lost, followed by the winner taking on the next boy, until there was a final winner among the five boys present. I worried about Frank's ability to move on from the sixth grade after I heard his plan.

"Forget it!" I said in a moment of bravado. "I'll do it."

"All right! Go get 'em, Boudreau," Frank said. With a fair amount of trepidation, I approached the porch with my boxes. Just as I was about to ascend the porch steps, I saw a shadowy something within my peripheral vision. It was Mr. Forgette, crouched alongside the porch, waiting to spring. Too late, I stopped as an enormous hand reached for me and glanced off my chest as I bolted away with Mr. Forgette in pursuit. I easily outdistanced the rather heavy, clearly out of shape Mr. Forgette, then I flew over the fence to ultimate safety from his clutches. As I did so, I heard Frank holler from the other side of the fence: "He'll never catch that long-legged Boudreau." Needless to say, my mother was unhappy with the phone call received from Mrs. Forgette, who now had an identity. Although forever busy with my brothers and sisters, Mom found time to dispense a few whacks around the back and shoulder with her quick hand along with a warning to leave the Forgettes in peace.

Spike found my punishment to be humorous at the least. A phone call to his mother would have meant a sterner response from his father in keeping with Mr. Dumbrowski's desire to raise Spike to be a man. A phone call to Frank's mother would have resulted in this conversation:

Mrs. Foley: Bill, you need to talk to your son.

Mr. Foley: Okay. Hi, son.

Although Mr. Dumbrowski put up with Spike's friendship with me – I lived three doors away – he much preferred Frank as Spike's friend because Frank's father was a prize fighting addict. Since Chuck Dumbrowski believed that every boy should learn to fight, he approved of Mr. Foley's efforts to teach Frank and all his friends the art of fisticuffs. Mr. Foley built an official boxing ring in his backyard. There, he ran bouts every Wednesday night between boys he would match up on the basis of age and weight. He was the referee. The fight lasted all of three rounds with oversized gloves, so it was unlikely that there would be anything but a draw; Mr. Foley was also the judge, the trainer, the ring announcer, and the maintenance man. All of this was more unusual because Mr.

Foley had only one arm. His day-time job was to sit in a shed near the tracks all day and step out with a stop sign every time a train approached his intersection. The story was that he got this plush job because he lost his arm in a railroad train accident of some sort. His lack of an arm did not deter Mr. Foley from his self-appointed boxing bout responsibilities, even the unlikely task of a trainer. He showed youngsters how to jab with the left hand – a hand he possessed – and to punch with the right hand, a hand that boxing students had to envision as he flicked the small piece of arm that was attached to his right shoulder.

There were two memorable bouts that summer evening when we were ten. The first one pitted "Potato Chips" Duncan, the grocery store owner's son, against "Newstip" Jackson (his parents owned the local newspaper distributorship). Potato Chips was cocky and confident, an accomplished street fighter. Newstip was a student of the arts; in fact, Mrs. Jackson sent him to a dance school for a short period until Newstip rebelled. Newstip was terrified, but he had something to prove, so he stepped into the ring with Potato Chips, who had determined to make short work of his opponent.

That night, we saw two distinct approaches to the art of prizefighting. Potato Chips' approach was to charge across the ring at the bell. Newstip was all about defense as he stood paralyzed a few feet from his corner with one glove over this face and the other glove stuck out in front of him. As Potato Chips dashed into the fray, he stole a glance toward the onlookers to appreciate who was there to witness the projected massacre. In that split second, he ran directly into Newstip's glove, a blow that landed directly on Potato Chips' chin. He crumbled to the mat; a knock-out in the very first round, in fact in the very first few seconds of the first round.

"...eight, nine, ten, you're out!" Mr. Foley declared as he helped Potato Chips regain consciousness.

The next memorable bout of the night featured my friend Spike Dumbrowski against T-Boy Bouregard. I have no idea how Mr. Foley came up with this match. T-Boy was bigger, older, and much tougher by reputation. Even his nickname, T-Boy, emanated from the many times his parents said of him: "That boy's a terror." However, Spike had taken a genuine interest in acquiring boxing skills. Long before he knew that he was going to have the opportunity to use his acquired skills, he had read and practiced in the basement of his home. He shifted his feet, he jabbed, he shadowboxed, he banged a punching bag – he was prepared. During the fight with T-Boy, he danced around him, he jabbed him in the face again and again, he dodged T-Boy's hay-makers; in short, he outboxed T-Boy for every minute of the three rounds. Of course, Mr. Foley called it a draw, but everyone knew that Spike was the clear-cut winner.

Spike, Frank, and I attended a matinee movie one Sunday afternoon. You could get in for a child's price if you were less than twelve years old. Although Spike still wasn't very tall, he carried himself as though he were older. The cashier questioned his under-twelve status. Spike whipped a birth certificate out of his pocket. He came prepared.

The movie house was crowded that day; the Al Jolson Story was playing. We hunted for three open seats and finally found them.

"Hold the seats for us," Spike ordered as he and Frank headed for the popcorn counter.

Along came two elderly women. One said: "Here are two seats."

"They're being saved," I said.

"Nonsense," one of the women said, "you can't save seats that aren't being used." They sat down, much to my dismay.

I went back to the popcorn counter to give Spike and Frank the news that we had lost our seats, but I was too embarrassed to tell them that I had been pushed around by two old ladies. "Two big guys came and took them," I lied.

The movie theatre was in an adjoining city, Cohoes, so we walked to get there, approximately two miles. However, a short cut did exist. Cohoes was separated from Waterford by the Mohawk River. There was a choice of two bridges to make the crossing. One was for cars and pedestrians, with a large sidewalk, and the other, which we called the high bridge, was for railroad trains. It was closer to where we lived and shortened the distance to Cohoes by a considerable amount of time and energy. However, the walking space was minimal, meant only for railroad employees who might have to work on the tracks or for employees or train passengers who might have to get off the train in an emergency. The bridge was constructed primarily of wood, with the walkway only wood. A few round parallel bars separated the walkway from a plunge into the Mohawk. A sign at the bridge's entrance clearly outlawed the use of the high bridge by pedestrians. My mother always cautioned me on the way out the door to the movies to "use the low bridge." So, of course, we used the high bridge to go to and from Cohoes. A special thrill was available when a train passed while we were on the bridge. The practice was to stand and hold on to the parallel bars as the train passed as the bridge shook somewhat violently from the train's weight and velocity.

Once, I was invited to go to the movies with my oldest brother and his girlfriend. It must have been Pinocchio or some other early Disney film. Ed was proud of his extraordinary balance. Sometimes, as a parlor trick, when I was about six and he was about 20, he would have me lay flat on my back while he stepped on and over my stomach. He did this without exerting any pressure on my stomach by somehow miraculously shifting his weight. To this day, I don't know how he accomplished that. On the day we crossed the high bridge – Ed, his girlfriend, and I – he climbed to the top rail and walked on it, a show-off stunt that could have easily plunged him into the Mohawk. I was amazed and terrified. His girlfriend was impressed and terrified.

As I indicated, I was one of eleven children, with Ed the oldest. When I was six, I was particularly proud of the fact that my four oldest brothers were serving in World War II. We had a banner with four stars on our front porch indicating this for all to see. That left me with one older brother, with whom I had no shared interests, and five sisters to spoil me. My closest sister, Beth, was The Princess. I suspected that some of the kids coming to the door to see me were there to catch a glimpse of Beth. The activity we shared the most, I guess, was Beth washing and me drying the dishes while engaged in singing the latest pop tunes.

But I digress. One of the kids from the public school was named Red Vozy. We liked Red. Sometimes he played touch football with us. He was always the quarterback and made us feel important when we caught one of his passes. Red's name came up one day from a surprising source. We had never seen a police officer in our town of Waterford. I suppose that there was a police force of some kind, but no policeman was ever seen in our particular neighborhood. But one day, as Spike, Frank, and I were sitting in our sewer curb location, a State Policeman stopped his car by us. We were amazed to see such a sight. A lanky State Trooper stepped from his vehicle and said: "You guys know where I can find Red Rosy?"

"Red Vozy you mean?" asked Frank.

"Vozy, yeah."

"No, we don't know him," Frank said.

Then Spike piped in. "Maybe we know him, maybe we don't," he said boldly. "Why do you want to know?"

The Trooper decided not to pursue it with us. Instead, as he turned to get back into the vehicle, he addressed Spike: "A kid like you will grow up and find himself in a prison somewhere."

"Wooooo," Spike said.

I marveled at his audacity and fearless manner. I wasn't about to give this authority figure any lip.

I'll mention one last incidence of our mischief-making that year that resulted in Frank doing himself in, very much to Mr. Foley's displeasure. Not unlike when he called out my name at an unfortunate time as I ran from Mr. Forgette, Frank, and Frank only, was at fault for identifying himself to mischief victims. It was all because of Frank's pride in his hand-writing ability. Unlike the rest of us, his handwriting was something to behold – large, flowing letters with a flair. One night, after pounding numerous cars with snowballs from our favorite attack point, Frank felt the need to urinate. We were having much too much fun for Frank to run home to his bathroom. We were in the relatively secure area provided by Mr. Denault's back yard, presently full of snow from the latest 14-inch snowstorm. He couldn't resist demonstrating the flourish of his signature on the fresh snow pile. Remarkably, he had the foresight to not capitalize his first name, allowing one unbroken stream. There it was when motorists came looking for snowball throwers, his name emblazoned in the snow in pee-yellow for all to see. Now that I think about it, that may not have been the only time when Frank was a source of excrements flowing from his body. For example, as kids we all spit, probably as a result of watching baseball players. However, Frank played with his spit. He would let the material emanate from his mouth in a long string, then suck some of it back up into his mouth, then let it go again, yo-yo style, before finally fully discharging the accumulation. It was both fascinating and disgusting to watch.

I had a BB gun when I was ten years old. It was formerly owned by at least one brother, maybe two or three of them. The mechanism was faulty at best. When I fired the rifle, the BBs more or less just rolled out. Occasionally, however, it expelled the ammunition and hit the target. It was very unpredictable.

There was a time when the gun worked too well, but I was deeply ashamed at the result. To this day, I'm not a hunter of anything alive, but I shot at a sparrow on a telephone wire that day. The bird was hit by the BB but didn't drop; instead, it hung upside down clinging to the wire. Suddenly, I realized that I had caused pain to a living thing that did not want to die. With reluctance, I told Spike and Frank about my regret at shooting a bird.

"Hunting is a sport," Frank said. "Years ago, people killed animals to eat and survive, but now it's just a sport. The bird had no brain and no soul. Good shot."

Spike didn't agree. "I understand how you feel. There are people who go out of their way not to step on an ant. If you feel bad about killing a bird, just don't do it again."

I began to feel better because of Spike's words until he said: "Three Hail Marys and you're off the hook."

Nevertheless, I did have use for the gun on one additional occasion. Spike, without the knowledge of the sometimes ineffectiveness of my gun, thought it would be a wonderful idea to have a shooting competition. Frank saw dollar bills coming our way.

"Here's what we do," Frank said. "We charge a quarter for some shots. If they hit the center of the target, we give them a prize. We'll buy some cheap prizes that look expensive over at Woolworth's."

"Just like a carnival," Spike said.

"Ah," I muttered, "should we have them use their own BB guns?"

"Whatever they want," Spike said. "Or they can use one of ours."

"I have to tell you," I said, "that mine doesn't always work all that well."

"Then it will be just like a carnival," Frank said. "If they choose your rifle, what can we do? That's part of the throw of the dice."

Spike said: "Mixed metaphor."

"What's a meta for?" I asked.

"Are we linguists or are we carnival operators?" Frank said. "Let's get the show on the road."

"Wow," Spike said.

"Tell you what," Frank said, "Tony, why don't you spruce up your gun a little bit, maybe polish it."

"Frank," I said, "I think that you are going to grow up to be a carnival huckster."

We spread the word at school and in the neighborhood. Frank borrowed his father's dart target. I thought to myself that darts was probably the perfect sports activity for a one-armed man. Spike bought the giveaways but changed the concept in the process. He went to a trophy shop and negotiated a deal with the owner that allowed him to purchase a first-place, a second-place, and a third-place trophy, trophies that the owner of the shop had used for samples for years and had thought about replacing them when Spike suggested that that's exactly what he should do. Small problem that was ignored: One trophy had a man with a bowling bowl, one had a runner holding a football over his head, and the other was a baseball glove on the trophy with an inscription that read "Most Valuable Player." Details.

"I figure that the winners would rather have trophies than cheesy prizes," Spike said.

When the day of the BB gun competition arrived, we had wisely allowed Spike to set up the structure of the competition, remembering Frank's suggestion as to who would approach Mr. Forget's porch by throwing fingers.

"We have twenty-five contestants," Spike said, "so we'll have five at a time compete against each other. The winner of each group will move on to the final five. They'll shoot against each other for the trophies. Best three shots will win the trophies."

"How many shots does everyone get?" I asked.

"Five. How about that? Five, five, five, everything's five."

Most of the boys had their own guns. A few picked up Spike's gun or Frank's gun. Despite my spruce up, my gun was sensibly ignored. Of course, Spike, Frank, and I were the judges, so we stood precariously close to the target. Only the best shot of the five shots was the one used to determine the winner. In about a half an hour, we had our five finalists.

Hey, the entire competition was fun. We were excited about the finals. Then, one of the finalists made it even more exciting.

"I think my gun veers just a little bit to the right," Benny Samuels said. "I'm going to use one of your guns."

"Take anyone one you want," Spike said, pointing to our three rifles.

I felt that someone hit me directly in the solo plexus when Benny said, "I'll take this one." Mine, of course.

To make the competition even more intense, Spike determined that each of the finalists would take one shot followed by the next finalist taking one shot, etc. It came down to a final round of each shooter trying to better the best shots already fired. Surprisingly, Benny was in the chase with my rifle. My gun was cooperating. Then, as it turned out, Benny had the last shot. It meant either a first-place trophy (the bowler) or third-place trophy (the baseball glove). Benny intently took aim and fired the shot. The BB rolled to the end of the barrel, flew about three inches, and dropped to the ground.

I was embarrassed, but Benny said, philosophically, "Guess I didn't win." He didn't even complain about the gun.

Before we rewarded the trophies, Frank insisted on a meeting of the judges.

"We took in $6.25," Frank said, "and Spike paid $2.00 for the trophies. We've made $4.25. We're rich."

"Here's your third-place trophy," I said to Benny, "and you can have the BB gun, too."

"No thanks," Benny said, "you can keep the gun."

I tucked it deep in a closet and never used it again.

As Charles Dickens would say, all these things, and a thousand like them came to pass in and close upon our dear old tenth year of the lives of Spike Dumbrowski, Tony Boudreau, and Frank Foley. In many ways, that year prepared us for the rest of our lives.

TONY AT 13

Spike and I made it to the eighth grade at St. Anne's, full of ourselves. We knew at the beginning of the school year that we would be the youngest and brightest. Of course, that wasn't saying a whole lot since there were only seven students in the class, four girls, Frank, Spike, and me. Yes, Frank was now with us. He had some strange and unfortunate incidences while in the seventh grade. First, he kneeled on a long needle lying in the carpet of his home. That required surgery and time out of school. That was followed by whooping cough and chicken pox. A bad year for poor Frank. The bottom line was that the nuns thought it necessary for him to repeat the seventh grade. That's why we caught up with him, so he was with us in the seventh and eighth grades, although he was older.

Something else happened to Frank during that time. He became depressed and intellectually lazy during his string of health problems. Consequently, his performance in the classroom was lackluster at best. His lack of enthusiasm for his studies continued into the beginning of the eighth grade, but Spike thought he could help remedy the problem. Spike counted primarily on the fact that Sister Cecilia had no great knowledge of the subject matter. With great confidence, she stated facts that were simply wrong. He encouraged Frank to straighten her out. The more he prodded Frank into correcting Sister Cecelia, the more Frank gained confidence and interest in the subject matter. Before the year ended, Frank was in the driver's seat of each day's lesson. Spike and I suspected that Sister Cecelia knew quite well what she was doing. It is quite likely that her stumbling around with the lessons was simply a ploy that invited intervention. Frank did so well academically that school year that he finished third, just a percentage point behind me. Of course, we were both outdistanced by Spike who was still amazingly adept in his studies.

This was a period in my life when I was terrorized by females, save my mother and sisters. I did not have a single conversation with Marilyn, Rita, Helen, or Bernice. This affliction was not possessed by Spike who seemed to know all the right words at all the right times. He had a comfortable, breezy manner of talking to boys and girls. Marilyn was particularly terrifying to me. One time that year, I passed her walking in the opposite direction a mile or so from home in a shopping area. She smiled at me in recognition – we had been in school together for our seven years. I attempted a "hi," but my larynx froze right along with my facial expression, shocked to see her. In retrospect, I marvel now at how easily boys and girls of that age talk to each other today. Spike not only could talk to the four girls in class but he chatted with them, played tricks on them, and told them jokes. I was merely an observer, not a participant, in these activities.

Although all four girls might have been considered "cute," Marilyn, in my opinion, was an outstanding beauty. I was sure that she, eventually, would be the love of my life.

That's why it was so shocking to hear from Spike that he had kissed her in the shadows of Durant's grocery store one evening after the other kids had left for home. That, alone, was unnerving, but there was more. He had dropped in at her babysitting site a few days later at her invitation, and they had necked! I was crushed. But Spike's triumph meant nothing to him. Instead, he encouraged me to partake of some of the same generosity displayed by Marilyn. He went out of his way to arrange a situation where Marilyn and I were in the same place of his original conquest a week or so earlier. Understandably, the set-up was unsuccessful since all I could manage was a few inept words of conversation, not really a conversation at all. I almost made the bold move, however, of touching her hair when Spike returned to the site. Marilyn gave me a "See ya" and left. Spike asked: "Did you do it?"

"No, no," I said. "Almost."

A few days later, Spike told me that he had a heart-to-heart talk with Marilyn and she confided in him that the guy she really liked was Frank!

Spike was glib for a thirteen-year-old. He was proud of his ability to chat. Some evenings, when his parents weren't home, he would call Marilyn or Rita or Helen or Bernice. It didn't really matter which one. I would sit and listen to him carry on long conversations, just to prove he could do it. He went further than that to demonstrate his oral prowess. Occasionally, he would dial a phone number at random. If a man answered, he'd hang up. If a woman answered the phone, whether she happened to be thirteen or thirty-three, Spike would find a way to initiate a conversation.

Sometimes, he would demonstrate to me how he could take over a conversation within a group. We would be hanging with, oh, seven or eight guys who were sometimes carrying on one conversation but mostly carrying on a number of conversations simultaneously. "Watch this," he would say to me. "I'll have them all listening to what I've got to say." Sure enough, he would enter into the midst, say something provocative or even interesting. All eyes and ears were directed to Spike.

Even Spike's mother was intimidated by Spike's loquaciousness. She was just mild-mannered anyway, even without the influence of a stern, cranky husband and now a son who wouldn't shut up. Spike respected her well enough but showed off his ability to embarrass her in front of his friends. When I was in his house waiting for him, he especially liked to use the bathroom without closing the door. You heard the splash of urine falling into the water and the flush of the toilet.

"Isn't that terrible?" Betsy Dumbrowski would say to whatever friend happened to be there: "A boy of his age!"

"Please close the door when you are in the bathroom, Spike," she would say.

"Sure, Mom, sure," Spike would reply. "Anything you say, Mom," he would say as he patted her on the back patronizingly.

Spike also knew how to get things done. St. Anne's had no outdoor basketball court, and we couldn't get into the gym except during school and during evening basketball games. Spike, Frank, and I decided we needed to have a hoop to shoot at during the summer and in the evenings when weather allowed. We were told by the nuns that there was no money for additional recreational activities. This was Spike's kind of challenge. First, he got Frank to get his father to buy the hoop - no blackboard, just a hoop. That was successful. When Bill Foley wasn't planning prizefights or holding up signs at a railroad intersection, he enjoyed watching basketball. All three of us were worth watching. I could make jump shots from almost anywhere near the basket, Spike could make three-point shots before three-pointers were part of the game (his counted for only two points), and Frank was not reluctant to mix it up under the boards. He also had an unorthodox hook shot from either side of the basket with either hand. But we wanted to stay sharp during the off-season. We needed to get that hoop mounted. That's when Spike went to work on Mr. Duval, a man who enjoyed playing games with kids – basketball, touch football, and basketball. He could hit a baseball a mile into the air. We would stand underneath the high fly ball and do our best to catch it. Most of the time, the ball landed a few feet away.

"Tell you what, Mr. Duval," Spike said. "If we could get the lumber, would you help us build a backboard?"

"Sure," the amiable and helpful Mr. Duval said, "but you'll need a post also."

"We'll have everything we need by this weekend," Spike told him.

That night, Spike led us on an expedition. Up behind the area where we lived, in a field that used to be nothing but hills of bush and wild strawberries, there was the beginning of a spate of new homes under construction. Some of the homes were being built by the owners who were not particularly professional in construction or in security of materials. Numerous pieces of wood of all sizes lay unprotected near the homes in process. In the dark, we helped ourselves to sufficient lumber for a backboard and then found the perfect post, although it would have to be shortened. Frank carried an armful of lumber for the backboard. It took both Spike and I, one of at each end, to carry the post. As we made our stealthy exit, a neighbor shouted at us: "Hey, what are you kids doing with that stick?"

"That stick?" I gushed. We laughed so hard that we about dropped the post. Some stick. It was a solid four by four that was about ten feet long.

Mr. Duval asked no questions. He showed up with his tools and helped us put up our own basketball hoop on school grounds. The nuns never asked about it either.

Beyond those hills of newly constructed and construction in process homes, we had other adventures while in the eighth grade. Three of them had to do with a bottomless water hole that sat above the Cohoes falls. For some reason, it was called Second Hole. Where and if there was a First Hole was beyond my understanding. However, it was a beautiful place to swim. Pristine water flowed slowly out of there in unnoticeable increments and then rushed down the massive falls. To get to Second Hole, we had to walk past the hills to a steep cliff that descended to our natural pool. Everyone, with two exceptions, used the same, well-traveled, reasonably safe path down the cliff.

One exception was when Frank found a spot at the top of the cliff that appeared to be an edge of the cliff but in fact had an extended plateau of six feet or so just on the other side of the apparent edge. Frank loved to find new visitors to the swimming hole. As he made his way through the hills, he would relate to the first-time users all of his personal problems, mostly fictional, and how he wasn't sure he could take it anymore. Then, at the plateau site, he would suddenly bolt for the apparent edge, giving every impression that he was leaping off the cliff (while landing on the plateau). That was great drama until the day that he missed the location. Frank didn't realize his mistake until he reached the very edge. In an acrobatic move, he reversed his direction only to land on his stomach with his legs dangling off the cliff. That was the last time he employed that prank.

The other time that someone disregarded the walk-down path was when Regis Lafavre decided that he wanted to find an alternate path to the swimming hole. He started down this new path only to freeze somewhere in the middle. He couldn't take the next step down, and his arms and legs would not work to allow him to make his way back to the top. Spike and I were with him that day. We had watched with some awe but also with some concern when he started his trek down the unfamiliar section of the cliff.

When we realized he was stuck, Spike took action. He sent me to run the several miles back to our neighborhood to find someone with a rope who could help us. He remained to keep

Regis calm, convincing him to hold on, that help would soon be there.

I knocked on five doors before I found an adult at home. He responded to my plea for help by rummaging around until he found a rope that might do the job. He was a bit on the heavy side, so it took us a while to make our way back to the cliff location. When we arrived, we saw a fire truck at the top of the cliff. While I was running for help, someone in a factory across the other side of the falls had called the fire department. A fireman had descended on a rope, tied it around Regis' waist, and other firemen had pulled them both to the top. The next day, the Cohoes American Newspaper reported a daring rescue above the falls. Spike and I and the huffing, puffing man I brought to the scene were not mentioned.

The other incident involving the swimming hole is a painful and embarrassing memory for me. No one ever touched the bottom of the hole, even the best swimmers who held their breath a long time and attempted to find a bottom. I was not a very good swimmer for some reason. I went swimming enough; I just was never all that comfortable in the water. My swimming consisted of a single stroke forward, around, and back to the water's edge. I was in the middle of this routine when suddenly, two guys splashing around me, I lost my rhythm: I forgot how to swim. I swatted at the water in a very unconventional way and had the beginning of some very panicky thoughts. Even then, I was either too proud or too ignorant to call for help, but Spike saw my predicament in an instant. He jumped in, restored my balance with a tire tube that was sitting idly by the edge, and directed me out of the water. We never talked about it as saving my life, but that may have been the case. In fact, we never referred to the incident after that. Spike was very conscious of my pride and let me keep it.

Our friend Mr. Duval found the time to play games with us and erect our basketball hoop even though he and his wife had three young sons. Since they lived only a few doors away from us, my older sisters were in demand as baby sitters. On one black day of my life, however, my sisters were not available. Mrs. Duval asked my mother if I could do the job. It wasn't very difficult; the kids behaved well and went to bed early. My greatest fear was that Spike would hear that I was a baby sitter. I swore my family to secrecy. However, the Duvals rather liked the idea of my sitting their kids. Consequently, they passed over my sisters, and I became the regular sitter. It was impossible to keep this a secret. Spike asked if I had to wear a skirt when I sat for the kids, whether I read the kids bedtime stories, and if I was going to take on other babysitting jobs in the neighborhood. What Spike didn't know was that babysitting added materially to my sex education. After the kids were in bed, I read Mrs. Duval's racy novels. We didn't have books like that around our house.

The Duvals were also responsible for my meeting – well, almost meeting – Sandy. I had heard that Mrs. Duval had a niece who occasionally visited. Somehow, she always managed to pop out the door when I passed. She would be checking the mailbox or placing an item on the porch, or picking something up off the porch, or even sweeping the porch. We eyed each other but never spoke a word. She was to reenter my life a few years later when I not only spoke to her but dated her in my senior year of high school.

Spike, of course, not only noticed her appearances on the front porch but stopped to introduce himself. When I saw him casually leaning against the porch banister in deep conversation with Sandy, I found another route to get to where I was going. The shyness long remained with me.

Spike and I went to work at thirteen. Mr. Poorman was a butcher and ran a grocery store just down the street from Duncan's grocery store. At the time, the supermarkets were just beginning to put such operations out of business. He hired us both to work for two hours after school all week and all day on Saturday. Our job, our only job, was to deliver groceries on bicycles that Mr. Poorman owned. The bikes had large baskets attached to the handle bars that provided sufficient room to carry two to three bags of groceries. In a way, he was way ahead of internet retailers. Customers in the neighborhood would call in orders to Mr. Poorman who would also make recommendations and prepare the finest cuts of meat, and we would deliver the groceries free of charge. I'm not sure why, but that's all Mr. Poorman asked us to do. We didn't retrieve the groceries from the shelves, wait on customers, or even sweep the floor. He did it all himself, save for making deliveries, our job. Consequently, we had to amuse ourselves while waiting for a delivery order. Typically, we did so by lounging in the space just inside the front window. Spike was very good at making himself quite comfortable. Often, he would borrow rolls of toilet paper or paper towels to provide a headrest as he sprawled and napped for everyone to see as they drove past.

The kindly Mr. Poorman had absolutely no problem with our resting between delivery trips. Actually, he seldom spoke to us other than to send us off on a delivery and to caution us to go straight to the address of the recipient and to return as soon as possible. The only problem I had with those instructions was that I was terrorized by a large collie that barked and chased the bicycle wheels as I passed. Consequently, if I had to pass in that direction, occasionally I took an alternate, longer route. When Mr. Poorman glanced out the window and noticed that I was headed in a long-way direction, he chastised me. Spike came to my rescue. He told Mr. Poorman about the vicious animal that might put the order in peril. Instead, he offered to go with me for the next trip. Spike not only talked to people, he chatted with animals. He stopped, talked away to the large collie, patted it a few times, and then sent it back to the front step of the home before continuing on. I still took the long way around after that.

Other than giving us delivery instructions, the only other time Mr. Poorman talked to us, it seems, was to offer us a delicacy while he was butchering.

"You boys should have some of this," he'd say. "It's delicious. It's blood pudding."

To this day, I don't know what blood pudding is nor do I want to know.

TONY AT 14

With all the kids in my family, and with my father supporting us all with a job as a supervisor in a toothbrush factory, I belonged in the public school system after grade school. I was enamored, however, with a private school that had uniforms and a football team, LaSalle Institute. I knew that Spike's father, determined to raise his son as a real man, would want Spike to attend this military school. Frank's father liked the idea for Frank; the school had a boxing team and basketball also. Since I was bringing in fourteen dollars a month (three fifty a week) at Poorman's Grocery, and I knew that I could still do the job while in high school, I suggested that my family could afford to send me there if they could pay the additional two dollars a month to meet the sixteen dollars a month tuition. They agreed even though they knew quite well that I was going to spend some of the fourteen dollars a month on something or other every month and that there would be other expenses, little things like books, etc.

Spike and Frank held out of sports until basketball season. I wanted to play football and was anxious for the tryouts. However, the tryout instructions specified that it was necessary to have certain equipment, one of which was a jockstrap. It is truly remarkable now to remember that I had never known the need for one in grade school and, as far as I knew, I did not absolutely need one for high school. Since I didn't want to make my parents spend yet more money, I didn't go out for the team.

Not long after that, I learned that my parents had to make the buy anyway because a jockstrap was required for our physical education classes. This was one of the many times in my young life when my timidity prevented me from enjoying life to the fullest. On the other hand, this fault may very well have prevented me from many heartaches and disappointments.

The three of us were happy at LaSalle except that we discovered that we were not as amazingly bright as we thought. There were many more students in this class, and some of them displayed brilliance that we had not witnessed at St. Anne's. In addition, our nuns never told us about the worlds of Algebra and Latin. While Spike continued to master linguistic skills, even he struggled with these new mathematics challenges. Outside of those minor difficulties, we enjoyed the uniforms, the bigness of the school, and teachers who whipped us into shape physically and intellectually.

The teachers were Christian Brothers. They ruled with a heavy hand. It was not extraordinary to have a brother whack a hand across the face or head if the student wasn't performing well. They took absolutely no guff from any student. Brother Damian was the fiercest. He would clobber any one for good reason or on a whim. Tom Sweeney sat at the desk next to mine. He had a strange habit of falling asleep and slipping off his seat onto the floor. It was a riot! Unfortunately, Brother Damian took Tom's penchant to slip onto the floor as a personal insult. On one such occasion, just as Tom was bringing himself up off the floor, Brother Damian landed a whack with the back of his hand that sent Tom sprawling. Big mistake. Tom came up swinging, much to Brother Damian's surprise. One punch was all Tom got in before Brother Damian retreated with a command for Tom to proceed to the principal's office post haste. Both Spike and Frank were in the classroom that day. We all vowed afterward that if Brother Damian struck one of us, we would attack him together and pummel him, regardless of the consequences. As for Tom, he was no longer a student at LaSalle, but he never regretted retaliating.

In the middle of the school year, I woke up in the middle of the night with a significant pain in my side. I toughed it out, but by morning, I was doubled over in agony. My mother called the doctor my father was seeing at the time for a rash. Dr. Henson was a general practitioner. He practiced alone and he treated everyone for everything. He even delivered babies. Most amazing of all was that he made house calls! Some doctors actually did that at the time. He quickly determined that I had appendicitis. He called the hospital, and I was admitted. The kind doctor also sensed my concern that I was going to be in a ward with children. "He's very tall," he said on the phone. "He'll need an adult bed." Spike and Frank visited me at the hospital often during a ten-day stay, but Spike spent most of the time in deep discussion with several young nurses or nurses' aides.

I lost about a month of school. This created two problems: one, I was completely in the dark on Algebra and two, I was not able to go to work at Poorman's Grocery Store. How on earth could I expect my parents to come up with sixteen dollars for that month's tuition? Once again, my personal advisor, Spike, came to my rescue. Without asking me, he made an appointment to see the principal, Brother John. He explained my predicament, including a totally – well, at least greatly – exaggerated description of my family's financial situation. He was convincing that I was the kind of student who would bring pride to the institution and that if the school were to lose me because of my family's financial state, it would be a tragedy of great proportions. He was so persuasive that Brother John called me in to announce that my tuition would be waived not only for the month that I missed classes but for the remainder of the school year.

Of course, I missed the basketball season, but Spike became a star of the freshman team. Between the eighth grade and the beginning of basketball season in high school, he grew six inches! His future three-point shot, formerly accomplished with two hands, was changed to a one hander. He was dead on with a high percentage of shots. Frank played well also with his penchant to bang bodies under the hoop. When opponents double-teamed Frank, Spike made them pay from the outside. When they stepped out to guard Spike, Frank was unguardable in the paint. So, while Spike and Frank were basking in glory, I was recovering, catching up academically, and taking charity. I couldn't wait for the year to end so that I could move on to the public school for my sophomore year.

As it turns out, I didn't have to wait that long. Two weeks before the end of the school year, Brother Damian told the class that a sentence could not begin with a conjunction. Spike pointed out that he was wrong.

"That's the general rule," Spike said, "but this prohibition has been ignored by authors from Anglo-Saxon times onwards. Sometimes an initial and or but will draw attention to itself and its transitional function." Brother Damian was not Sister Cecelia. "Don't ever contradict me with your smart-mouth misinformation, Mr. Dumbrowski," he said. As he did, he reached over and slapped Spike across the face. "That's a reminder never to do it again." Spike rose menacingly to his feet. As one, Frank and I moved toward Brother Damian. We charged. Brother Damian ran. We were suspended for the last two weeks, but the understanding Brother John granted our credits and suggested that we might want to further our education elsewhere next year.

All three of us transferred to a small public school after our less-than-spectacular freshman year at a military academy. The Waterford High School faculty welcomed us, but the boys at Waterford High had attended school together since Kindergarten; they were a tight group. I was depressed because I didn't make the basketball team. Frank was also shut out to my surprise. I guess the coach was satisfied with the team he had. Spike was the lone pickup, and he played well although he was still the outsider when the passes were distributed around the court.

For me, it was a dismal year. I couldn't get into my studies; I spent a good deal of time daydreaming in the classroom, visualizing myself catching a touchdown pass, making thirty points in a basketball game, or hitting home runs. I didn't have a clue as to what was going on in the classroom. Miss Fleet, however, took me out of my doldrums. She wasn't one of my teachers; she was the guidance counselor. She learned early on that we shared a passion for the St. Louis Cardinals. I began dropping into her office each morning for a chat about the previous day's Cardinals game. I was always greeted with a smile and a firm handshake. Actually, once my handshake was not firm enough. She chastised me for it. Then she discovered that my grades were very average. She compelled me to take an I.Q. test of some kind, something that measured my potential. When it was determined that it was clear that I could do so much better, she pushed me to do so. So it was that one member of the high school faculty that woke me from my daydreams and turned me around academically.

Miss Desautel also did her part to bring me out of my shell. She was the French teacher. I knew a little – very little – French because my parents sometimes spoke Canadian French around home. However, I made no effort to learn the language; rather, I tried not to learn it, feeling that Americans should speak American, that is, English. Nevertheless, Miss Desautel appeared to like me, probably because of my French heritage.

Consequently, when the French Club put together a play for a school assembly, I was given the part of a French soldier even though I had no interest in acting and didn't audition for the part. The play was short, about forty-five minutes long, but there were only three of us in it, a senior who played a statue of Joan of Arc who comes alive, another French student who played an English soldier, and I played a French soldier.

Spike helped me to memorize the lines, but I was uncomfortable with the long lines of dialogue between the English soldier and me. Spike sensed my stage freight and had a solution: He would stand offstage with the script and whisper the words that I didn't come up with on my own. He was my personal prompter.

Thus fortified, I was more or less confident as the play began and progressed. Then, we came to one of the long passages that I had memorized word for word. I went blank. I looked at Spike. He had become distracted, staring at the Joan of Arc statue, fascinated that she hadn't moved a muscle. There was a long pause. In frustration, my next words were not in the script: "What the hell is the next line?"

The play was not a comedy; it was a serious, historical perspective, but my line brought the house down. I noticed, several years later, that I was not invited to participate in the Senior Play. Miss Desautel was unhappy with me, but I found a way to regain her favor. One of my older brothers had acquired a recording of La Vie en Rose, sung in French, from a friend in Paris. He gave it to me because he thought that it would incite some interest on my part in my French class. Miss Desautel was delighted when I gave it to her. Talk about shining the apple!

Spike continued to breeze along, getting As and gradually being accepted by the basketball team. However, he didn't forget his old buddies; we continued to hang together evenings, always exploring who we were and where we were going in life. One night, we walked all the way to Troy, a distance of about five miles, just to check it out. Along came a group of five high school boys, perhaps a year older than we were. Frank, ever the wise guy, made a remark about their general appearance.

"Look out. Here comes the Mafia," he said.

They turned toward us menacingly. Frank retreated behind Spike and me. One of the guys moved toward him. Instinctively, protecting my friend, my fist flew, striking the aggressor in the face, knocking him back. We were about to be pummeled out of our senses when Spike stepped forward with his hand up. We knew, of course, about Spike's vocal proclivities, but how he proceeded to talk us out of that situation was basically marvelous. By the time he finished talking at them, all five boys were convinced that the whole incident was a total misunderstanding and in fact we were in Troy to pay homage and learn from Troy high school students. Unbelievable!

TONY AT 16

During the summer preceding our senior year of high school, Spike, Frank, and I had jobs. Spike and Frank worked at the A&P, the only supermarket in town. I had a job at an ice cream and milk processor. I spent a good deal of the time in a winter coat in the freezer while the temperatures outside were eighty degrees or higher. I consumed much of what I saw, ice cream cups, creamsicles, fudgsicles. Good stuff.

Once a week, however, I assisted an old, crotchety guy with installing pipes for milk processing. Under his supervision, we would climb on ladders and affix a series of pipes in a complicated configuration. He was constantly annoyed with me because I didn't know the difference between a right-hand bolt and a left-hand one. "Right hand, right hand," he'd shout at me. He was certain that I was more of a hindrance than a help, and he may have been right. That's why I took great pleasure one week when he had been delayed on pipe installation day. Quietly and unobtrusively, I installed the entire pipe system on my own much to his shock and dismay when he arrived.

"Did you do that?" he asked, surprised.

"Yes, sir. Piece of cake," I said.

At the A&P, Spike and Frank were bored most of the time, leading to efforts to entertain each other. With the solid experience that Spike had in lounging at Mr. Poorman's grocery store, his opportunities expanded with the much larger supermarket. He delighted in showing Frank how he could toss together a very comfortable resting place made up of boxes and packages of paper towels. Frank, elevated to cashier status, performed whenever Spike was within ear shot. One day, he rattled off the products as he moved them across the scanner. "Manhole covers," he said when he came to the sanitary pads. He was fired on the spot, and Spike's dismissal took place soon afterwards.

Suddenly, in my senior year of high school, I woke up to new experiences – a bit of fame, girls, and some ambition. Frank was right there with me. Spike, as always, was a step ahead. We all made the basketball team for the last two years of school, but our senior year was the most rewarding. We scored mightily, won some big games, and received a great deal of attention. Somehow, I can still remember the sounds of the crowd as I sunk a jump shot just before the buzzer resulting in a come-from-behind win against St. Bernard's. Ironically, for a week or so after the game, it was not the shot that was remembered so well as the booming cheer of my older brother. He ran a barber shop just a few blocks from St. Bernard's where most of the kids from that school went for haircuts, so everybody knew him. He made more noise than anyone else throughout the game and then really erupted with that winning shot. That was my moment of basketball glory; nevertheless, Spike continued to outdo Frank and me, both academically and on the basketball court.

This was the year that I was motivated by and was able to respond to the cutest girl in school, a junior who I had noticed – as did everyone – when I was a sophomore. Still unabashedly shy, I attempted a call to Joanne, a la Spike, but lost my courage and hung up as soon as she answered the phone. Consequently, I was stunned when she called me to say that a group of students were going to the local roller skating arena and wouldn't I like to join them. I accepted the invitation immediately even though I had never set foot in a roller skating shoe. The result was humorous for everyone else, embarrassing for me, as I mopped the floor frequently with my body. When attempting to skate as a pair with Joanne, she warned me to let go of her hand if I were to go down. She had no intention of letting me take her down with me. The Holiday Dance, a kind of early prom, was the first big social event of the year. Joanne made it be known to all her friends that I was going to ask her to the event. When I heard this news, somewhere down the line, I was sure there was a misunderstanding, but, no, it was just a matter of my hearing the news so that I could make it a reality. When I asked her to the dance, she said: "Of course." But an unpredictable situation would emerge that would prove that Joanne was not in charge after all.

Frank was the only one of the three of us who owned a car. It was a piece of junk, but it was his. Spike had a date for the big event also, but Frank did not. Instead, he wanted to drive us, be our chauffeur. We readily agreed so that we could concentrate on the girls instead of the road. The idea of four of us squeezing into the back seat or one of us sitting up front with Frank did not appeal to Joanne. Besides, she wanted to go with Dan and Jan, her friends, with Dan doing the driving. In retrospect, Joanne's plan was certainly more sensible. My plan would call for either my sitting up front with Frank (not very friendly, Joanne pointed out) or crowding into the back seat when two of the passengers (the girls, of course) wore fluffy dresses that all by themselves took up an amazing amount of space. With each of us sticking to our guns, the date was simply called off. Joanne did no further planning that involved me.

While Spike breezed through girl friends with his talent for casual conversation, Frank and I had only infrequent encounters with the opposite sex. We lived vicariously through Spike who related every detail of every association with a teen-age girl. I did find, however, that my basketball presence made dates available for me if I wanted them – and if I wanted to spend money on such frivolity. Two instances come to mind.

Roberta came to the United States with her family from Portugal. All I did was offer her my sweater in the chilly air during a fire drill. That resulted in my being told numerous times through the grapevine that we were an item. I learned quite a bit from Roberta, least of which was a bit of the Portuguese language.

"Feliz Natal is Merry Christmas," she told me. I thought surely I could make use of that sometime in my adult life.

"But never use the word fork," she said. "It's okay in English but a naughty word in Portuguese."

Spike roared when I told him that. Only then did I realize the obvious.

The second incident involved my old classmate Marilyn. Yes, she was at the public high school, but I still hadn't had a conversation with her, much to my consternation and much to Spike's amusement. Marilyn was very popular with the boys in the class. I heard from others, including Spike, that she sometimes invited boys outside of an ongoing sports event to illustrate her "necking" techniques. I was astonished and jealous until I received one of those invitations while watching one of the Junior Varsity games. This time, my larynx didn't freeze; my entire body froze. She walked away, totally befuddled at my failure to seize the day.

Miss Fleet continued to be my link to normal social behavior, but it was Miss Gaynor who put me on a large stage to my amazement. During one of her English classes, she announced a regional oratorical competition. Students were to prepare a ten-minute speech on good citizenship with prizes to be awarded by the American Legion. About a dozen hands were raised, including those of Spike and Frank. I had no idea why I did so, but I raised my hand also. Miss Gaynor gave us the necessary rules after class and told us of a future date when students of Waterford High would compete, with the winner going to the enormous convention center in Saratoga to compete against winners of competitions among other high schools.

I worked diligently on a ten-minute address. I didn't have many ideas, but I heard Mayor Impellitteri of New York City say something about our country not having an iron curtain as did Russia but a voting booth curtain that protected our right to vote. I built on that, even incorporating those words, but I wondered whether I had a right to do so. Imagine my shock when we reached the deadline date for submissions. Neither Spike nor Frank submitted a paper. In fact, no one who raised hands on that fateful day submitted papers. I was the winner by default! I would have to compete in the regional contest without ever delivering my paper at my own high school. Now, I was really nervous. Miss Gaynor had me read the speech into a tape recorder. I had never heard my own voice until that day. I was dismayed; I thought that I had a much deeper voice. The real problem, however, was the prospect of competing in front of a few thousand people on a large stage in a gigantic convention center without any experience in speaking whatsoever.

Miss Gaynor invited Spike and Frank to come along for support and drove us the thirty miles or so to Saratoga. To make it worse, I was selected at random to make the third presentation although there were fourteen competitors. The first presenter was bombastic, speaking loudly and clearly, driving important points home. He was a wonderful speaker who obviously practiced and had won against other contestants. My preparation had consisted of carefully watching the priest deliver his sermon at Sunday Mass and reading a magazine article in the library about speaking. All I remembered from the sermon was that the priest used his hands a lot. All I remembered from the magazine article was that it was useful, occasionally, to take a step toward the audience to emphasize a point.

The second contestant seemingly had a photographic memory. He related some Colonial history event complete with numbers, dates, and percentages. I was next.

As I walked onto the stage, I was reminded by one of the judges that it was a ten-minute speech. He would stand to signal that eight minutes had lapsed and stand again if I were to go over twelve minutes. Any great deviation from the projected ten minutes would cost me penalty points. It occurred to me that maybe I could make a run for it, but that didn't seem practical. I looked into the audience and saw Spike giving me a thumbs-up sign. How could he rescue me from this bottomless water hole? Instead of memorizing points, I had memorized the speech. I began tentatively reciting the speech by rote. Suddenly, I lost my place, so instead of taking a step for emphasis, I took a step to try to remember where I was, then another step. Then, somehow, I picked up the thread but jumped over the part about the iron curtain and the voting booth curtain. I may have done so unconsciously because I was uncertain about my legal right to use Mayor Impellitteri's words. Having picked up my memorized speech at a later point, I realized that I didn't have much material left. I looked toward the judge. He was still sitting! I hadn't yet reached eight minutes and I had only a few memorized words left. The final sentence was: "I am proud to be an American." It was delivered this way: "I … am … proud … to be … an … American." As I said the last word, the judge stood. I exited the stage to a polite scattering of applause but with loud applause – and whistles – from Spike and Frank. I didn't win.

That spring, the three of us ran track. Because I could jump fences, which I proved with Mr. Forgette in pursuit when I was younger and because Mr. Forgette never came close to catching me, I competed in the high jump and the one hundred yard dash as it was then called. Frank thought that the two hundred would be a good event for him. Spike decided that a half mile – twice around the quarter-mile track – would be his best event. We didn't have the slightest idea how to prepare for these events. Our coach, a man who had been the basketball and track coach for over twenty-five years, had no interest in teaching us. We didn't practice because we didn't know that practicing was necessary. We assumed that all it required was running fast, and we could do that.

I quickly discovered that performing a high jump wasn't the same as jumping over fences while being pursued. I then found out that coming out of a starting block was a huge part of running a sprint. I was unsuccessful in both events. Frank quickly discovered that running two hundred yards as fast as he could go required some lung capacity. He, also, was unsuccessful. But Spike had the greatest flop of all. The eight hundred required running twice around the outdoor track. Spike bolted out in front of the pack with dazzling speed. He became confident when he noticed that he was running away from the other runners. After he had run once around the track, his legs became heavy and he could hardly breathe. As he began the second lap, one and then another runner passed him by. He struggled mightily to keep moving but his body and his spirit gave out. It had rained heavily the night before, so the ground off the track was muddy with puddles. As he tried to move his legs and body along the far side of the track, he gave out, stumbled, and fell into a muddy water puddle. As he walked, aching, across the center of the track after the race was over, Frank and I applauded his effort. I may even have given him a thumbs-up signal.

TONY AT 17

For Spike, there was no doubt that he was off to college. He thought that he would like to teach – a guaranteed audience for his continued loquaciousness, so he signed up at the local teacher's college. His father had put away a tidy sum for Spike's college education. Spike could afford to attend college while Frank and I had no thoughts of college. It wasn't in the family budget for either of us. We thought that a high school education would serve us quite well.

Frank and I landed jobs at the same bank as tellers after a few months of training in another department. As it turned out, Frank was a decent banker; I was the world's worst but not for lack of effort. In my very first week as a teller, a gentleman paid off a car loan with two checks that amounted to more than the loan balance. This transaction occurred in the middle of the day after I had placed one deposit after another aside to count later, so I wouldn't keep any customers waiting. I added the two checks, subtracted the loan balance, and gave the customer $1,019 in change. He looked at me in amazement, grabbed up the money, and quickly exited the bank. This gave me some pause, so I re-did the calculation. I had given him $1,000 too much in change. I had the man's phone number off his check, so I called him to point out my minor arithmetic error and to ask him to return the thousand dollars. There was no answer. And he didn't answer his phone for the rest of the day. That's when I summoned my co-worker, Frank. Together, we decided that I would close for the day not showing the $1,000 discrepancy. We would go to the customer's home and demand the money, we decided. At seventeen, this made perfectly good sense.

Before we made the fifteen-mile trek to the customer's house, we enlisted Spike for his assistance. Can you imagine our chances of recovering the money, with three teenagers knocking on a door and demanding the return of $1,000 mistakenly given in change? The man answered the door; he responded to our demands by saying that he did not receive $1,000 more in change than what was coming to him. But once again, Spike came through. Spike pointed out, lying, that his father was the Chief of Police. He said he'd rather not bring him in on this unless it was necessary to do so, but, in any case, he said, he was certain that it was a misunderstanding of some kind. Maybe he could re-check the envelope that I gave him with his change. Maybe, Spike said, it's in there and the customer just didn't notice. The man was probably ten years older than we were, but the seventeen-year-old Spike got to him. He said he would take another look. Lo and behold, the money was there after all. Once more, Spike proved that the mouth is mightier than the sword. The bank auditors never learned about the one thousand dollars that was missing for one night, but I determined there and then that banking was not my true calling.

That fall, while I worked at several other office jobs, and Spike attended his first semester of college, Frank stayed at the bank but joined the National Guard. His plan, eventually carried out, was to join the Army the following year. The Korean Conflict had ended a few years earlier, but it was clear that other problems were brewing in the Far East. Frank talked about the "opportunities" that would open for him if war broke out.

Spike, in the meantime, wasted his college opportunity. He discovered beer parties and had the mistaken impression that he could get by without cracking a book. Just before the semester ended, Spike announced that he was not going to flunk out. Instead, he was going to drop out. Spike's father, who had mellowed considerably and was now a mountain of patience, told Spike to get a job and start over at a different college in the fall. I was astonished at Chuck Dumbrowski's metamorphosis from garage grouch to paramount of understanding. I believe he let the reason slip out one day.

"Boys," he said to us one day while we were resting after a basketball scrimmage in his driveway, "Someday, you'll have to think about your financial future. Invest your money wisely. I've had a little luck in the market lately, so I'm retiring from fixing everyone's clunkers."

Chuck Dumbrowski's brother-in-law, who lived in the tenement above the Dumbrowskis, opened his eyes when he heard this. That may have been the only time I ever saw him with his eyes open. Prior to that time, when he stood quietly watching Spike's dad at work on the cars, it always amazed me how he appeared to be completely asleep on his feet. I suspect that until that time no one ever said anything that interested him.

Spike, Frank, and I continued to hang together that year although none of us was accomplishing anything significant. We had ideas but no means to pursue them. Only Frank was enthusiastic about one part of his life – his participation in the National Guard.

Spike, in his outgoing, casual manner, made friends in college even though he didn't remain with them at school. One of the places they frequented, although Spike was still under the eighteen-year-old legal drinking age in New York State, was Al's Bar and Restaurant. The bar was on the first floor in a two-story building. Upstairs, there was an apartment of sorts that no one had lived in for many years. Al kept some junk up there including a few barrels of pickles no longer meant for consumption. Spike thought that the upstairs would make a great meeting room for a club, so he started one and got Al to agree to let him and his friends use the upstairs apartment at no charge but with the responsibility to clean it up. First, the guys created a name for the club – the Brotherhood. Then they set about to enlarge the membership. One principle of membership was that all members had to approve new members; one veto would mean that a potential member would be rejected. Frank and I were the first two outsiders to be admitted. With Spike nominating us, we were shoo-ins. Others brought in friends also. Soon the membership of the Brotherhood was at twenty or so. Our first task was to make the club room livable. We did so by cleaning the floor, walls, and windows and hauling out all of Al's abandoned junk, including the pickles. There were about twelve of us who worked a long day to complete the job. After it was finished, because the club restroom was very small, we moved to Al's restroom in the bar. Most of the guys headed for the urinals. Spike and I washed first, much to Spike's amusement.

"Look at this," Spike said. Tony and I wash our hands before we touch our privates. The rest of you slobs take a leak with your dirty hands."

The clubhouse consisted of a poker table, a sofa, chairs of various kinds, a dart board, and a few waste baskets – all obtained from various home basements. It was, obviously, first class.

The Brotherhood had the following rules: One: Attendance at a meeting on the first Friday of the month was mandatory. Three misses in a year and you were ousted. Attendance before the meeting at a Catholic Mass was optional. Two: If you missed a meeting on a first Friday because you had a date, this was reason for immediate dismissal from the club. Three: The club was always open, but you had to pick up after yourself; we had no cleaning lady. Four: Any member could nominate a new member, but the new member had to be voted in by every other member, unanimously.

The main activity at the club was poker. We played late into the night, sometimes into the early morning. There were some reading materials available; Spike stole magazines from the local drug store. He could afford to buy them, but stealing them was more entertaining.

We tried to maintain some semblance of order during the first Friday meetings. We elected a President, Vice-President, Treasurer (although there were no dues and the club owned no money), and a Secretary. We also followed Robert's Rules of Order to the best of our accumulated knowledge. At one meeting, a member suggested that we use the considerable musical talent and knowledge among our group to obtain a band and to sponsor a dance at St. Bernard's Hall. We would spread the enormous profits from this venture among some favorite charities. We discussed the ins and outs, the benefits and downsides, the risks and rewards for a good two hours. At the next meeting, our Secretary, Jack, reported on this discussion: "Check dance." A few years later, in the Army in Germany, I met with Jack one evening. He was stationed in the same city. We wrote to the Brotherhood members about plans for our next meeting, possibly in Czechoslovakia. Jack's report in the letter: "Check Czechoslovakia." The dance, incidentally, was a big success.

Being a member of the Brotherhood always guaranteed a friend to call for a movie or whatever. The concept was workable, although cliquish, of course. The fact is that we took in any one who was interested despite the apparently ever-increasing difficulty to obtain all votes for a new member. One of the new members, voted in unanimously of course, was Tom Sweeney – he of the fall-asleep and fall-off-the-chair La Salle student. I hadn't seen him since the Father Damian incident and his expulsion, but one of the new members nominated him, and there he was on the new member ballot. Of course, I voted for him although I was certain that he would nap during our monthly meetings. He didn't disappoint me. However, he seemed to come out of his semi-unconsciousness occasionally when the meetings dragged by saying, "Meanwhile, back at the ranch..."

TONY AT 19

At nineteen, I was in a dead-end job as an office clerk at a valve manufacturing company. I had succeeded, however, in obtaining twelve credit hours at a local community college, primarily because Spike, who still was not working very hard at it but was passing, told me that I would never get anywhere professionally without that "sheepskin." Frank joined the Army but was not yet due to report to duty when it occurred to me that I didn't want to wait around for a few more years to get drafted, a thing of some certainty at the time. So, as Frank was enlisting, I volunteered to be drafted earlier under the then-current policy of drafting eligible young men for the military when they became twenty-two or twenty-three. And so it was that Frank and I went off to Ford Dix, New Jersey, at the same time and were assigned to the same unit for basic training. Spike presented me with a copy of the Unabridged Work of William Shakespeare that he had stolen from the public library as a going away gift. How could I turn down such a meaningful gift? The stolen Shakespeare went with me to Dix; I was confident that no one would track it down there.

Frank was considerably more "gung-ho," as they use to describe it, than I was when it came to Army life, and I was admittedly a bad influence. For example, we noticed that roll call was being made in the morning but not when we reassembled in the afternoon. One afternoon, we were scheduled to do some competitive calisthenics. I suggested that we make our way to my car, which I wasn't supposed to have on base, and to go to the local shopping center. There we were pretending that we were civilians again, even though we were dressed in Army fatigues, when Frank froze.

"What?" I asked.

"Coming down the escalator," Frank responded.

I looked quickly. It was our company commander.

"Move!" Frank ordered.

We dodged the bullet. Apparently, he never saw us. Even if he did, I'm sure he would not have recognized us as being his company's soldiers. Surely, however, he would have been puzzled to see two soldiers in fatigues strolling around the shopping center in the middle of the afternoon.

We took various tests during basic training for placement after basic. One was to determine if we were intellectually qualified to apply for Officer Training School. The hitch was that, if you applied and were accepted, you had to become Regular Army and increase your stay in the Army for an additional year. Frank had enlisted for three. He applied and was accepted for officer training. I was satisfied to remain a foot soldier and keep my stay in the Army at two years.

SPIKE AT 21 and 22

After I dropped out of the first college I attended, I found that college wasn't all that difficult. I enjoyed most of the classes, even did a little Shakespearean acting. Actually, I thought that memorizing lines for Shakespeare was easier than memorizing class material. There was something about the flavor of the language, much of it antiquated, that filled my memory cells without much effort. I was an English major and that's the reason that I was drafted to be Othello in a college production put together by the Shakespeare Literature class. While most classes were enjoyable, even interesting, I didn't really apply myself to any of them except for this class. The material from other classes came so easily that I didn't work very hard at any of it, but Shakespeare was a special challenge, a turn-on.

The best news, however, was that Ellen was to be my Desdemona. I had known Ellen since high school, even dated her a few times, but the real fire wasn't there because she appeared to have no real interest in me. It wasn't that she had a greater interest in some other guy; she was serious about her future as a teacher and didn't have time for frivolity. She was so concerned about getting admitted to a good college that she worked harder than I ever did. She wanted to teach high school English. That's why she found herself in an elective with me in college, and that's why she was cast opposite me in Othello.

Although we didn't call them dates, we spent a great deal of time together during six weeks of rehearsals. We practiced our lines but also chatted, walked in the park, and hit Steak N' Shake. Some time, somehow, we became closer than either of us suspected. The three presentations of Othello over a single weekend sealed the deal.

I can't say that I was a great Othello, but I did my best. Actually, the role fell to me because no African Americans in the class were willing to take it on. So there I was, a Caucasian Moor with a voice that should have been much deeper for the part but wasn't. We decided that the audience simply had to accept me as a Moor just because I was so costumed.

I had no concerns about my dialogues and actions with Iago, but there were two scenes that did make me uneasy, both violent scenes. As you'll remember, because of Iago's lies, Othello becomes incredibly jealous. In one scene, I slap Desdemona across the face, and near the end of the play, I strangle her. Because I was becoming more and more enamored with Ellen, neither action was very palatable.

We worked on the slap scene during the rehearsals, attempting various methods that would look like a slap and sound like a slap. No matter what we tried, it looked phony. Finally, Ellen said, "During the performance, just hit me. I can handle it."

"I don't want to do that," I said.

"Hit me," she said. "Really, just hit me." *I really better not*, I thought. *She'll never forgive me.*

But hit her I did. Three nights in a row, I whacked her across the face. Every night, there was a discernible groan from the audience.

The strangling scene wasn't so bad. As long as I was careful to appear as though my fingers were applying pressure on her throat and didn't get caught up in method acting, we were all right. A major part of that scene, of course, was when I kissed her goodbye as she lay sleeping just before I strangled her. Those kisses were awkward during rehearsals but passionate during the shows. *Man, I like this acting stuff,* I thought. I was in love.

Some say that I used my persuasiveness, my gift of gab, to make her fall in love with me, but Ellen says it happened the first time I ever slapped her across the face on stage. I think that she's putting me on. Once we decided that we could not live without each other, we set a wedding date, a close one, four months later. I didn't have to choose between Tony and Frank for best man. Neither was available to be in the wedding. Both were serving in the U.S. Army and not able to obtain leave for the big event. I feel confident that they were both in shock after they received my letters giving them the wedding news.

During that first year of marriage, Ellen was the perfect wife, I thought. She went to work as an English teacher in the local public high school, which helped provide funds to survive during my first year of law school. Better yet, she shaped me up, gave me the incentive to study harder in law school than was my practice in college. She was ever vigilant, also, that I didn't fall back. Law school classes consisted of three hours a day with plenty of work to do after class. However, one day I found myself caught up with assignments after putting in about twelve hours of classes and doing assignments every day of the week up until Friday; I was caught up or even ahead of schedule. It happened at about 4:00 p.m., so I thought I would relax a little by watching American Bandstand, a television show I had never seen. It was fascinating with current singing stars appearing on the show and teenagers crowding the dance floor with all of the latest moves. In the midst of this television watching, Ellen arrived home.

"That's great. I'm stressed out all day with high school students who really don't want to learn and you're lounging around watching teenagers dance."

Then came the follow-up:

"Good, Hon," she said. "You need to take a break once in a while. You've been working awfully hard."

That was my girl. It was also the last time that I tuned in to American Bandstand

TONY AT 20 AND 21

Spike, Frank, and I stayed in contact over the next few years through the U.S. mail, long before easy access cell phone calls and text messaging, but we went our separate ways. Spike was cruising through college, satisfied to do as little work as possible but still maintaining a middle-of-the-class academic record. Frank became a Second and then a First Lieutenant in the U.S. Army. I was sent to Germany as a Private First Class to serve as a Battalion clerk for a Military Police outfit.

The very first week I arrived, I witnessed the death of a member of my battalion. Two MPs, dressed and ready for their shift on the job, began to discuss fast draws, just like old time Westerns. I was the only other person in the Recreation Room, casually reading the Army newspaper, Stars and Stripes. One of the MPs was a New Yorker, with a distinct accent. The other was a Mississippian. When he spoke, there was no doubt about his Deep South upbringing. It was on the third quick draw contest, after the first two had been won by the Mississippian by the blink of an eye, when the New Yorker, trying harder, pulled the trigger of the assumed unloaded weapon. The noise resounded throughout the small room. My eyes shot up to see the shocked horror on both faces as the Mississippian dropped to his knees, blood spurting from his chest. As the New Yorker gaped at the unexpected result of the dual, I bolted to the Mississippian who had now fallen forward into a puddle of his own blood.

Of course, I could do nothing for him. Much of what happened immediately after that is muddled in my mind, with other soldiers running into the room, some screaming for help, a whirlwind of emotions. The following day, as battalion clerk, I typed the letter written by Colonel Porterhouse, the battalion commander, to the soldier's parents in Mississippi. An investigation followed over the next few weeks, and I was called as an eye witness. Eventually, the death was ruled as accidental, but the New Yorker was sentenced to the stockade for six months for unauthorized use of a weapon.

Fortunately, my Army career had much happier moments after that tragic incident. The job wasn't difficult, a little typing, a little filing. This gave me a good bit of time to familiarize myself with Army rules and regulations – mostly looking for loopholes. I was also the first to see general announcements coming from Regiment Headquarters. One involved the formation of Army track teams. The deal was that a soldier could go on special duty competing in track for a period of three months. Why not, I thought, remembering my less than glorious high school days; surely I could do better now with the knowledge that training was necessary to success.

We had an oval within the barracks complex. The entire post was guarded, believe it or not, by German guards, hired primarily for public relations purposes. I have no idea why we didn't simply have our own battalion soldiers provide guard duty, but World War II ended only ten years before this time, so someone, no doubt, thought that it would help to improve community relations if German civilians were hired for this job. I decided that I would train a bit for my targeted event – the four hundred meter dash – by running that oval late at night. My first effort at training was interrupted when, apparently, I startled one of the German guards.

"Halt!" he said with a perfect German accent.

"The hell with you," I said out loud. Why should I stop my race preparation because some German employee ordered me to do so? Then I heard the distinctive sound of a barrel being released. Click! I came to a screeching halt.

Tryouts were at the stadium in Berlin, Germany, where Jesse Owens frustrated Adolf Hitler's dream of super athletes by breaking Olympic records as Hitler looked on in 1936. Our base was about an hour away from Berlin, and one of the other guys who wanted to try out had a car to get us there. Unfortunately, we misread the schedule of tryout events. Instead of arriving at Noon, when tryouts began, we were there at one o'clock. The four hundred had already been run. So as not to waste the trip completely, I entered the next scheduled event. I had no idea how really long 3,000 meters was. Remember that we ran yards, not meters, back in high school. A few trips around the track perhaps? So, I jumped in. Breezing to a lead during the first lap, I remembered Spike's high school experience and slowed down to a slower pace, then a very slow pace, then a virtual walk as the race continued and continued. Why on earth didn't I ask about the length of this race, I thought, chastising myself for sheer stupidity. My feet and legs got heavier and heavier, and the other runners began to pass me one by one to the point that I was dead last and still didn't know when it would all end. Finally, I stepped off the track and gave it up. (A few days later, I saw one of the competitors in that race at the PX, and he recognized me. "Why did you quit?" he said. "I was following you; you were doing great.")

There was only one event left, one I had never tried, the pole vault. I didn't even have an idea how to hold the pole. Nevertheless, a kind overseer of the event said he was sure I could do it if I tried. Thus bolstered, he gave me a quick lesson, and I gave it a try. To my amazement, I was able to pull myself off the ground toward the goal posts, or whatever they were called. On my third try, I cleared the hurdle and was offered a spot on the regiment team. Knowing that I was an imposter and would never beat anybody in competition, I turned down the offer.

The battalion commander made a better offer a few weeks later. He received notice that a Little League needed to be formed for children of Army personnel stationed in the area. He asked if I wanted to take some time off regular duties to organize a Little League. The offer came with instructions and money to buy equipment. After holding tryouts, obtaining managers, and buying uniforms, bats, and balls, we were ready to go. We had a draft process to form six teams, and we were in business. We were one manager short, however, so I signed on as the Yankee manager.

I'm no dummy. I selected my battalion commander's son as my centerfielder and my company commander's son as my left fielder, but my best selections were a ten-year-old shortstop, a twelve-year-old third baseman, and a twelve-year-old first baseman. Both of the older boys could reach the fences with their thundering blasts. The ten-year-old handled everything up the middle with great precision and success. On the other side of the coin was Billy who was small, uncoordinated, and afraid of the ball. I wanted every boy to play, of course, so I planned to put him in right field when our team was way ahead or way behind.

I still had to report for roll call and had some minimal duties, but I had it made, considering that this was Army life. One evening, the Master Sergeant made an announcement: "Cancel any plans that you have for this evening. This barrack is a mess. We're going to scrub the floors and walls even if it takes all night. Of course, that doesn't go for you, Boudreau. You have Little League practice." Somehow, this did not enamor me with my fellow enlisted men.

It was a great season. Third baseman Jimmy and first baseman Hal led the league in home runs, Robbie, our shortstop, was consistently wonderful in making really tough plays and making hard plays look easy, and the other boys contributed with singles and hustle. Perhaps the biggest challenge was keeping the boys keyed in. Every once in a while, I would see an outfielder admiring butterflies or studying the ground. Tommy was one of those boys. He would man the outfield with all of the concentration of a squirrel looking for his next nut. He looked everywhere but at the batter. It goes without saying, then, that a few balls skipped by him before he had time to react. That's when I developed a watch-the-ball exercise for all the boys but with Tommy primarily in mind. You know those signs at ballparks that say no pepper allowed? I was never sure what that meant, but I knew that pepper meant hours of hitting ground balls and then fly balls to the boys, especially Tommy.

One day, much to my pleasure, Tommy showed up with a new glove, a birthday present. It had a wide, deep pocket. Tommy was fascinated at how he could go get the ball, coming in or going out, and the ball would land and stay in his new glove. Hallelujah!

Billy, however, was yet to get the hang of things. He tried and he tried, but somehow the ball always dropped somewhere in his vicinity but never into his glove, not to stay anyway.

The Yankees were tied for the league lead with the Red Sox when we reached the final two games of the season. In the penultimate game, solid play by the Yankees with a sparkling catch by Tommy and two home runs each by our big hitters resulted in a victory. Unfortunately, the Red Sox won their game also. And lo and behold, the final game of the season was to be against the Red Sox. That became the championship game.

I had seen the Red Sox pitcher who was to pitch that day a few times against other teams. I assume that no one was lying about his age, but the kid was a bruiser. He stood about six foot three at twelve years old, so he was intimidating. Scarier yet was his fastball. Really, they could have put a full-grown man out there and we would not have been more intimidated. He made short work of Yankee hitters in the early and middle innings because they couldn't see the ball and react quickly enough. At the same time, we stayed in the game, making excellent defensive plays. Tommy in the outfield and Robbie and Hal in the infield stopped most everything the Red Sox players hit. The thing about a really fast ball thrown by a pitcher is that if a batter can get around on it and meet it with the meat of his bat, the ball can go a long, long way. That happened when third baseman Jimmy did just that. We led one to nothing.

It stayed that way into the bottom of the ninth with the Red Sox batting. We were hanging on for life. I had not put Billy in the game but was feeling guilty for not doing so. He sat on the bench looking at me in a way that meant either please put me in or please don't put me in. I decided to give him his chance. We needed three outs. I prayed that no ball would be hit to right field. The first hitter hit a screaming line drive at Jimmy who caught it. No problem. The second hitter hit a wicked one at Robbie. Over and out. Still no problem. Then the trouble began. The next Red Sox hitter successfully bunted to get on base. The next batter hit one so long and hard that even Tommy and his magic glove would not get to it, but he did get to it on the first bounce fast enough to keep the first runner from scoring. With men, then, on second and third, their clean-up hitter came to the plate. I began to think about the little speech I was going to make to the team after the game, something about what a wonderful season they had and how courageously they had played in this final losing cause.

Instead, the hitter slammed one into right field, long and hard. Billy waved at the ball as best he could and then, suddenly, the world stood still. I blinked. The ball was in Billy's glove.

I knew it before Billy knew it. He looked at the ball safely ensconced in his glove with genuine astonishment. Final score: Yankees 1, Red Sox 0.

* * *

Because I was in a Military Police battalion, I was trained to fire a forty-five, but I was in a headquarters company, so carrying a gun was not part of my modus operandi. However, I was given the opportunity to compete in a shooting competition that was organized by our company commander. Captain McMillan assumed that he was the second best shot in the battalion. He knew about Colonel Porterhouse's expertise with the forty-five, so he had three trophies made – first place, second place, and third place. Not so paradoxically, the second-place trophy looked better than the first-place trophy. I was allowed to compete because I asked to be part of this event right along with nine active MPs and, of course, the colonel and captain. We had a warm-up practice the day before the real competition. I knew that I wasn't that hot of a marksman from those days during basic training when I learned to shoot an M1 and a carbine, and I squeezed off a few practice shots with the forty-five that demonstrated my lack of expertise. That's when the MP next to me on the shooting range made an observation.

"Hey, you seeing that target all right?" he asked.

"I guess," I responded.

"Here," he said, "try my glasses."

I had a pair of Army-issued glasses that I never wore. They were issued because it was clear that I needed glasses when I took the vision test upon indoctrination into the Army. That was the first professional eye test of my life, and it was the first time that I realized that I had been seeing objects at a distance in a blur. Nevertheless, I didn't want to be bothered with the Army-issued glasses, so I tossed them in my foot locker where they stayed. On the day of target practice, however, it was clear to me that I became a much better shooter by looking through the glasses of my neighboring MP on the target range. And so it was that, the following day, I competed in Captain McMillan's shooting competition with spectacles on my face and with the convenience of seeing the target sharply. The colonel had the highest score as expected. The captain did well also but not so well as the battalion clerk. I shot the eye out of the target sufficient times to win the second-place trophy. I don't believe that Captain McMillan ever forgave me, even though I had made his son the lead-off hitter for the Yankees.

I was so proud of my marksmanship that I volunteered to fill in, if needed, on active MP duty. That opportunity came a few weeks later. It was the one and only time that I went on patrol. It was not to be my most glorious moment. My partner for the night, Ted, took the call: a fight at a local bar involving American servicemen. What we saw as we entered the bar was at least twenty young men pounding each other. Tables and chairs were overturned, some of the men were on the floor wrestling and punching, some of the men were hammering opponents toe to toe, and a few men were lying on the barroom floor, victims of knockouts. Ted's whistle blast could be heard throughout the establishment. For a second, everyone stopped the battle except for one young man who hurled a bottle of beer in our direction. It passed within an inch of my head. I drew my weapon.

"Put that away," Ted barked.

"This bar is closed for tonight," Ted roared as I meekly re-holstered my forty-five.

Being in Germany was a breeze, and obviously I had soft duty. I took advantage of leave time also to see some of Europe. I had the opportunity to take a bus trip to Paris, saw some winter Olympics in Cortina d'Ampezzo, and visited Vienna with friends. The most remarkable trip started with an invitation to get a ride to Venice with Robbie's parents and then go on from there on my own. I took a train to Rome (crowded and smelly with bockwurst sandwiches), on to Nice and the Mediterranean, and finally to Paris.

Of course, I was the typical tourist, snapping pictures, gawking, until I was approached by another American soldier on leave.

"Look," he said, "I don't know if you would be interested but the truth is, we have one date too many."

"What?"

"My friend and I met these three women from London. We want to go to dinner and maybe dancing, you know, whatever, but it would be nice to have another guy. Are you interested?"

My first thought was of the money in my pocket, rather on the slim side.

"Well, I guess so," I said, "but I don't have a lot of money."

"Just spend what you can," he said. "We really need another guy."

I agreed to meet them at a restaurant at 6:00 p.m. Knowing that I had to guarantee that I would have sufficient funds to get back to my post where I was stationed in Germany the next day, I went to the railroad station and bought a ticket. I had already paid for my lodging for that night, so, starving aside, I was now in a position to spend the remainder of my funds on this date that fell in my lap. The young woman turned out to be very nice and quite attractive. We had a nice evening, the six of us, and when we ended the date, we exchanged addresses.

Tired and now broke, I arrived at the railroad station and boarded what I thought was the correct train to my station. Along came the conductor who woke me to see my ticket. To my horror, I was on a train making its way through France to Switzerland, not the train headed for Germany. My communications skills in French, as you might remember, were minimal, therefore I was unceremoniously booted from the train since I did not have the money to buy another ticket. There I was in Nancy, France, alone and broke. I considered hitchhiking, which would have been difficult at best considering the possibility that I might not be able to communicate with anyone kind enough to pick up a young man who was obviously an American. Plus that, I really didn't know how to get to Germany via roads. Finally, I made my way to the American consulate with hat in hand. The man in charge explained to me that he wasn't provided funds for this sort of thing, but he would lend me $20 for a ticket. He also mentioned that I wasn't the only American soldier he had encountered with this problem. That took a bit of the sting away knowing that I wasn't the only soldier stupid enough to get stranded on leave for lack of funds.

Ten days before I was due to return to the United States to be honorably discharged from the U.S. Army, I received a letter from Spike. He regretted that neither Frank nor I were available to be in the wedding party, but he had married a young woman who he had dated in high school. This would have no impact on his plans, he said, to attend law school. He had obtained a remarkable grade on the Law School Admission Test and had been accepted despite his very average college performance. Significant financial assistance would come from his new wife's success in finding a well-paying job and Chuck Dumbrowski's agreement to pay Spike's law school tuition. A day later, I received a letter from Frank. He was on his way to Vietnam.

SPIKE AT 24-27

Whether it was married life or a decision on my part to get serious, my law school experience was a very good one. I graduated second in my class of forty-five students. Ellen must have known that I was going to wake up from my long academic nap when she married me. She told me that I was capable of much more than I had shown in college. It turned out that she was right.

I was fascinated by the study of law from the beginning. We were warned by teachers early on that one-third of this class of sixty freshmen would not survive the first year. There was no way that I was going to let down either Ellen or my father who was quite willing to spend some of his savings on my future. Fortunately for me, my reasoning process matched the approach needed for law school. Law school students who survive and receive good marks are those who can look at both sides of every issue with objectivity. Simply memorizing material, no matter how well, will not lead to law school success. I read and listened with the necessary objectivity and, consequently, had near-perfect marks at the end of the first year while fifteen students received notices that they had failed. In my junior and senior years, I was recognized generally as one of the best students and was appointed to the Law Review.

None of this shocked my loyal friend and supporter, Tony Boudreau, who was still in the process of obtaining a college degree by attending college on a part-time basis. Tony also married as soon as he returned from the Army, a lovely woman named Barbara. He didn't need a father to pay his college tuition; he had Veterans' Educational benefits that paid the way. However, he had a full-time job and attended college in the Evening Division. It was in my senior year of law school that I made a suggestion to Tony.

"Think about law school," I said to Tony. "I think that you could get in even before you get a college degree if your LSAT is high enough. Will your veteran's benefits extend to law school?"

"I think so," Tony said, "as long as my college combined with law school is considered the pursuit of one degree."

"I think you should give it a shot," I said. "Someday, maybe we can practice law together." Of course, that comment was just to encourage Tony a bit, but I thought *Who knows, maybe we will practice law together some day.*

There were two wonderful developments that year involving my friends Tony and Frank. Tony blistered the LSAT, and he was accepted at Albany Law School even before he had a college degree. I knew he could do it. He planned to work full-time while he was attending law school. That is something that no one did, but Tony had a job that had flexible hours. He could work around his law school classes and – better yet – he could study on the job. Anyway, that was his plan.

The other great news was the return of Frank from Vietnam. He was now a Captain and was assigned to training soldiers scheduled to go to 'Nam. During that time, he took lessons in speaking Vietnamese. We wondered why he would do that after the fact until he told me in a letter that he had volunteered to return to Vietnam within the year. Of course, I had an educational deferment, and Tony had already put in his two years of easy duty in Germany.

I graduated second in my class and was Editor of the Law Review. During that senior year, I wrote an article for the Law Review that I was certain would impress every researcher on the subject for years to come. I called it The Unsolicited Creative Idea: A Copyright Complexity. That title alone, I thought, would gain me perhaps national exposure. It was published, and I have no doubt that it shows up once in a while for some lawyer doing an extensive search on copyright law. Unfortunately, I discovered a few years later that an unsolicited creative idea was not a copyright problem at all but a patent problem. Oh, well, maybe I wasn't so smart after all. Nevertheless, I knew that opportunities were going to be mine upon graduation. My high ranking earned me a number of offers. I took the one that surprised everyone. Instead of going to work for a prestigious law firm where I could earn significant dollars right away but not have any important assignments for a while, I opted to go to work as an Assistant State's Attorney for little money but almost immediate trial practice experience.

I was one of twelve Assistant State's Attorneys in a large office in Saratoga County headed up by long-time State's Attorney John Hirshman, a humorless, dedicated prosecutor who was an excellent lawyer as well as a good manager. He assigned me to DUI cases. That meant that I would be in court two days a week for starters. Typically, DUI offenders pleaded guilty. We usually had evidence that we didn't have to use because of the guilty plea, consisting of a police officer's testing by breath or blood that the defendant had a blood alcohol content of .08 or more, the statutory limit for driving. One by one, the defendants would appear. In most cases, I would let the judge know that the People would offer fines in lieu of jail time for a first-time DUI offender in exchange for the guilty plea. The judge then would fine the defendant, order a DUI evaluation, and send him or her to a victim impact panel, a demonstration by victims or family members of victims of drunk driving crashes of the reality of losses caused by such offenders.

Mostly, the process was routine for me while sometimes traumatic for the offenders. Occasionally, however, I got to try a case. A defendant would plead not guilty, claiming that he or she was not drunk despite evidence to the contrary. Sometimes, the defense attorney would challenge the stop, saying that it was without cause. Sometimes, the claim was that the alcohol test or the blood draw was inaccurate. These not guilty pleas usually took place when the defendant had a prior DUI or prior DUIs because repeat offenders were looking at harsher sentences if found guilty. Sometimes, the offender was a politician or other public figure. Then that individual would hire the best possible lawyer in hopes of beating the rap. Less than three months after joining the State's Attorney's office, one of those cases occurred, and it was a sensational one. A sitting Associate Judge was charged with a DUI.

Judge James Crowley was pulled over by a police officer after he was seen swerving from side to side along a rural road. He refused to cooperate when the police officer ordered him to take a field test – walking a straight line and standing on one foot. He insisted that he had a bad knee. He also refused the breathalyzer test. That refusal meant that he would lose his license for three months automatically, but he would have a right to challenge that suspension, and his refusal would make it much more difficult to prove that he was drunk. Nevertheless, the police officer arrested him for DUI based on his fumbling around to find his license and the strong odor of alcohol on his breath. The police officer, who had been on the job for less than a year, was not intimidated by the judge's position on the Bench.

At first, I was surprised that I had been assigned the case. Then I saw the obvious: I was expendable. If anyone were to incur the wrath of a sitting judge, it might as well be the new kid. Nevertheless, I was pleased to have the opportunity. After several pre-trial hearings in which the defense attorney, Ron Wright, unsuccessfully attempted to get the charges dismissed, the case came to trial before a jury. Arresting Police Officer Clay

Thornton was the first witness. Of course, he related why he stopped the defendant and what followed.

"The defendant, Judge Crowley, struggled to locate his license and insurance card," he said.

"Did you ask him to exit the vehicle," I asked.

"Yes. He staggered as he exited. I found myself moving backward as a strong alcohol smell reached my nostrils."

"Did you ask him to take a DUI field test ?"

"Yes, but he refused. He said that he was a judge and that he knew the law."

"What did you do then?"

"I placed him under arrest and took him downtown. I wasn't about to give him special treatment because he said he was a judge."

My next witness was Amelia Ryan, an eye witness to the DUI arrest. The defense attorney was well aware that Mrs. Ryan was to be called as a witness, but there didn't seem to be much concern about this particular witness.

My questioning began: "Mrs. Ryan ..."

"Granny."

"I'm sorry," I said.

"Granny," she said. "Everyone calls me Granny. I don't answer to Mrs. Ryan."

"Okay, Granny, tell me how it is that you saw the arrest of the defendant."

"Well, I saw the lights flashing from inside my house. I walked out to the porch to see what was happening. The police officer stopped the driver right in front of my home."

"The street in front of your home is a two-way, two lane street, is that correct?"

"Yes, and his car was heading to my left across the street so that I had a good view of the driver where he was stopped."

"And what did you see?"

"I saw – and heard – the police officer asking for a license and registration. Then I saw the driver kind of hanging out the window like a puppy dog as the officer was talking to him."

"What did you hear the officer say?"

"He was asking whether he had been drinking. The driver kind of mumbled. Look, there's no question about it. He was drunk as a skunk."

Of course, Wright objected to this opinion and the judge sustained the objection.

I continued: "Have you ever seen a person who was drunk, Granny?"

"My, yes, many, many times. My late husband got that way too many times, always on paydays."

"And how would you compare what you saw of the defendant's condition to your late husband's drunken episodes?"

"The defendant was worse. He couldn't talk right, he couldn't hold on to his license, he trembled. He was a mess. That man was drunk, no doubt."

I turned my witness over to the defense attorney, hoping that he would ask the questions I anticipated. He did.

"How old are you, Mrs. Ryan, ah, Granny, I mean?"

"That's okay, Honey. Granny it is. Anyway, I'm eighty-nine and never been sick a day of my life except for the measles when I was a kid."

"I see. Have you had your eyes examined in the last year?"

"Get 'em examined every year. Twenty-twenty. Love carrots. I'm a modern miracle when it comes to my overall good health."

"Granny, can you see that gentleman in the suit seated in the last row in the courtroom?"

"You mean the one with the charcoal suit and red tie with white stripes, the man with the sandy hair?"

"Okay, very good. And I take it that you have excellent hearing also?"

"You bet, Sonny. I can hear a whisper in the woods."

The defense attorney did not put Judge Crowley on the stand to testify, knowing that the judge could not be forced to incriminate himself. He then made a spirited closing argument that the prosecution had failed with our "flimsy" evidence to prove that the defendant was illegally intoxicated. In turn, I argued that the testimonies of the police officer and Mrs. Ryan (but I called her Granny in the closing argument) clearly demonstrated that the defendant was drunk. I also pointed out to the jury that the defense gave no other reasons for his behavior when he was stopped.

The defense attorney had been very careful not to seat anyone on the jury who had ever been in front of a judge or had ever been accused of any driving infraction. We wanted to be certain that some jury member would not want a conviction simply because he had it in for judges. Few around the State's Attorney's office thought we would win this one, but we did. The judge was convicted of DUI, fined, had his driver's license suspended, and was ordered to attend a victim impact panel, just like every other guilty DUI defendant. What's more, the Professional Ethics Committee was asked to review the incident to determine whether the judge should continue on the Bench. I had my first trial victory and a great deal of local publicity.

Tony, now in his first year of law school, was ecstatic when he heard the news.

"Is this the future State's Attorney?" he asked on the phone. "Great job, Tiger, but, hey, you're not the only one shooting for glory. I just received a letter from Frank. He's on his way back to Vietnam."

FRANK AT 26

All I could see around me was blinding lights and smoke. Who knows how many types of weapons were being employed? Grenades, certainly. Bazookas maybe. Plenty of small arms fire. And advanced armaments that could remove a head in an instant.

Battlefield methods have changed considerably since World War II when masses of men attacked from beachheads and, of course, since the Revolutionary War when British soldiers marched toward the Colonialists and, when ordered to do so, dropped to their knees and fired rifles. We had learned from the Korean Conflict that we had to fire at lights, that the enemy was not always visible. We had also learned to conceal our troops, to fire from cover, any cover we could find. There was no way to determine the strength of the enemy. All we knew was that we were engaged.

My job as captain of a company was to keep our forces entrenched but ready until we could determine what our chances were for victory in this one deadly skirmish. I had determined early on that I would be there with my men, always at risk but definitely in command. Along with a cadre of soldiers, I was positioned slightly to the rear and right of where the main action seemed to be taking place. I was in contact with my lieutenants by radio while attempting to analyze the full specter of the battle through binoculars and through feedback from my officers.

Every few minutes, I was reminded of the proximity of danger as I saw explosives or saw bullets rip through a bush or strike a tree in my vicinity. Then, suddenly, it became even more real when I saw a soldier fall within ten yards of where I was. Although I'm ashamed to admit it, my first thought after that fatality was to move away from the action to a safer position. Immediately, however, I dismissed the idea. I was where I was supposed to be, in the thick of it. My mind was racing. I knew that, like any combat soldier, I was frightened but had to put that aside. Fear of death in these circumstances was a given, but I had been trained to do a job, to take the risks that were involved.

"Stay low, Captain," the sergeant near me said. "They may be honing in on us."

Sergeant Riley was a good one. He was, thankfully, typical of the tough, hard-nose Regular Army men I had in my company. He had served in Korea and, like me, volunteered for a second go for action in Vietnam. At that point, I doubted the longevity of either one of us. I took another long look through the binoculars. Most of the retaliatory fire appeared to be coming from one area.

"Time to move your men," I barked into the two-way radio at one of the company lieutenants. "I need to soften up a section at about ten o'clock from where you are. We'll cover from the middle with all we've got for about four minutes. Let's do it in exactly three minutes. I'll get the mid-section platoon on the program and confirm."

"Yes, Sir," came the reply from the lieutenant.

I immediately radioed the lieutenant designated to create cover. "Lieutenant, we've advancing from your left. In exactly two minutes and forty seconds, I want you to direct a barrage of fire at twelve o'clock from your position. Got it?"

Right on schedule, the enemy's middle received a pounding while the designated platoon rapidly advanced. "We're here," that platoon lieutenant announced. "Not much resistance. I think we have the bastards."

Now, I had to get closer to the action. The closer I could get, the better I could dictate the appropriate effort to close out the attack.

"Let's go," I hollered to the soldiers around me.

Sergeant Riley stayed right with me, but he cautioned me again. "Better stay down, Captain," he repeated.

I drew my forty-five. I wanted to add some fire power of my own. As I moved toward the middle of the conflict, the sergeant said it again, this time he was giving an order. "Stay down!"

Then, suddenly, I saw a shadowy but evident figure: a North Vietnamese soldier. Instantly, I fired my forty-five one, two, three shots. The figure went down. For the first time in my life, I had killed a human being, but I didn't have the time to ponder the moral aspects because new lightning fire and explosives surrounded us. To my horror, I saw Sergeant Riley go down, blood spurting from his chest.

Immediately, I dropped to one knee, but continued to fire until my revolver was empty. I reloaded as quickly as I could. One of the soldiers near me took a closer look at Sergeant Riley from the ground and made an instant conclusion: He was gone. The soldier sprang to his feet to continue the battle.

We're there, I thought. My company was giving them all we were getting and then some. Most surprising of all to me, I appeared now to be in the center of the action. Then, directly ahead, several more North Vietnamese soldiers appeared. Once again, I fired. This time, I may or may not have taken another life, maybe two. Most likely, these soldiers were hit with a barrage from my men. I was so sure that victory was ours that I took a few more steps forward. That's when it happened – a burning sensation on the left side of my head. It sent me reeling backwards. Oddly enough, there was no pain in the first moment, but I knew it would come eventually. I felt the muscles in my face tighten, not entirely sure that I still had a face. Multiple emotions seized my very being. Was I about to die? Had I been hit elsewhere besides the head? I felt every nerve react to the invasion of my body from whatever hit me. I saw the splattering of blood on my uniform and on the thicket around me. That's the last I remember of the battle. Now darkness seized my brain. In that instant, I was sure that I had joined Sergeant Riley as a fatality of the war.

When I began to perceive light, it ended five days of nothingness for me. At least that's what a doctor told me as soon as I was able to understand that I was laying in a hospital bed. Miraculously, I could see, but, understandably, my hearing had been impacted. As the doctor talked to me, he spoke loudly and used multiple gestures. At first, I thought there was something wrong with his hearing, not mine, but it didn't take me long to come to the correct conclusion: his voice was so distant because I could hardly hear.

"I'm alive," I said to him, astonished that I had survived. Then, I thought, God, I must look like a corpse even though I'm not one yet.

"I'm going to give you the news and then let you rest," he said. "I understand that you won your battle, but you lost some good men in the victory. You don't look so hot, but we're going to be able to make you prettier. Give us time. You were hit multiple times, primarily in the neck, shoulder, and skull area. You're a hero, Captain. We're going to do everything we can to make you whole again." I couldn't say a word. I tried to thank him, but the effort to formulate and mouth words was too much. I opted to return to a deep sleep once more.

Over the next few weeks, during the hours when I was awake, I begged for and received pain medication. Intermingled with the sleep and the consciousness and the semi-consciousness, I was under the knife again and again. Along the way, I secretly wished that I had succumbed to the wounds on the battlefield. I couldn't imagine what I looked like and didn't want to know. I envied Sergeant Riley's quick departure. I was certain that I was grotesque, although the doctors and nurses kept reassuring me. But I could see it in their eyes. Finally, I became less pessimistic and more curious. I asked to look into a mirror. Once again, the doctor who had first brought me out of my five-day coma was there.

"After you're all healed from the initial wounds and the first set of surgeries, we'll see to it that you're satisfied with your face. We can do wonders for you, so don't get discouraged with the first look. Maybe we'll make you look like Gregory Peck. How would that be?"

"Any chance you can make me look like Frank Foley?" I asked.

"I think that we can come pretty close to that, too." He answered. As he spoke, he gently placed a large mirror in front of me as I sat up in my hospital bed. To my astonishment, the image in front of me was almost the appearance I had before the injury. As expected, though, the skin looked discolored and stretched. My left eye was semi-closed. My left ear looked more like a nose than an ear. I looked quickly to assure myself that my nose was still where it should be and not attached to the left side of my head.

"The ear still needs some work," the doctor said, still speaking loudly and gesturing by holding on to his own ear. "Hang in there, Captain," he said. "We're not going to let you down."

TONY AT 26

Spike was a rising star. The State's Attorney wanted to keep him on board, so he made him his First Assistant. Surely, that would keep him for at least a few years, he reasoned. I was a law school senior, looking to the future.

Both Spike and I continued to attend Mass at St. Anne's, although neither of us still resided within the parish parameters. Once in a while, when we were at the same Mass, we stopped for coffee at a local restaurant. We were both at Mass on the day that Monsignor O'Byrne asked for prayers.

"I have been notified by Mr. and Mrs. Foley that their son, our own Frank Foley, has been seriously wounded in Vietnam. We have no other information at this time. Please pray for Frank now and keep him in your prayers today and in upcoming weeks as he fights for his life in a hospital bed in Vietnam."

I was stunned. After a short prayer, both Spike and I exited the church, knowing that the other would be there.

"My God, I had no idea," Spike said. "Had you heard?"

"No," I said. "I'm in shock. Do you want to go over to see his parents?"

"Yes, let's do that," Spike said. "Maybe we can get a bit more information. I hope they're up to a visit from us."

When we arrived, they genuinely were pleased to see us. They related how they had been informed of Frank's injuries by a telegram and then a phone call from a First Lieutenant who served an as information officer. He had been very reassuring that Frank would survive the injuries but would be undergoing some surgeries and would be returned to the United States as soon as it was practical to do so. As we sat and drank coffee in the Foley kitchen, I thought of Mr. Foley's long-standing interest in pugilistic endeavors. It occurred to me that he beamed just a bit with pride coupled with his concern for Frank's welfare. They had been told of Frank's insistence that he be directly involved in the heat of the battle. Mrs. Foley did nothing to hide her concern. She was obviously apprehensive. She would not be satisfied, she said, that her son was going to be all right until she could see for herself. She choked back tears as she wondered aloud if Frank was indeed going to ever be the same again.

Spike, as always the magic tongue, eased the concerns of the Foleys by reminding them of Frank's resiliency, his toughness, and his ability to overcome by recollecting some of the exploits he shared with us when we were all younger. This resulted in a smile or two from the Foleys, and, once again, I was proud of both of my friends. When we left, Spike made the Foleys promise that they would keep us informed of Frank's progress. We both offered our assistance in any way that we could provide it. I'd like to think that Frank's parents felt just a bit better as a result of our visit.

Frank was much in our minds as Spike returned to his prosecutorial duties and I returned to my studies in anticipation of graduation and the challenge of a bar exam.

TONY AT 27

Braver than most, I didn't look for a job with an established firm or try to obtain a job with a government entity after I graduated from law school and passed the bar exam. Instead, I took a big and probably foolish leap. I hung out my shingle; I opened a storefront law office to learn the practice of law on the job. It would be a general practice of law, taking on any problem that walked in the door. I was confident that if I did this while I was young, my mistakes would be forgiven and, better yet, there would be plenty of help from older, more experienced lawyers, judges, and clerks who would think me pathetic and "just a kid."

It wasn't surprising, then, that the first case to come my way involved a relatively small matter, at least it was small to me, not so small to my client. It involved a $3,000 car repair bill. Mrs. Thornton, a 60ish widow, had paid a part-time mechanic the money to repair her car. (Of course, I remembered all those days seeing Spike's father working on cars in his garage.) Mrs. Thornton's part-time mechanic said that the transmission had to be replaced; that was the only way to go. After she paid the bill and picked up the car, she continued to hear strange noises emanating from underneath the hood. She took it back to the mechanic who told her not to worry, that the new parts were just "settling in." That's when she took the car to a second mechanic who told her that she still was in possession of the original transmission.

Open and closed, I thought to myself. I'll put Mrs. Thornton on the stand, then the second mechanic. If the defense puts the defendant on the stand, I'll remind him that he's under oath, just like in the movies. But I was getting ahead of myself. First, I had to file the complaint and serve the summons on the mechanic. Since I wasn't in a position to hire a process server this early in my practice, I decided to do it all myself.

Mrs. Thornton knew that the mechanic's full-time job was at a valve manufacturing company. I went there with my complaint and my summons to accomplish personal service. First, I stopped at the office to let his employer know that I had an important reason to see the mechanic for just one minute. Could I see him while he was on the job? Very kindly, the employer's representative told me that she would call him to the office as soon as he could get away from operating equipment. I waited patiently for him to walk through the office door. Naturally, I was a bit apprehensive since I had never served a summons and had no real idea how anyone who is so served reacted to the service. When the door opened, I saw a guy who could have played center for the Chicago Bears. He was enormous. I thought that, surely, I was a dead man.

"Sir, you are served," I said.

"What the hell is this?" he shouted.

I didn't answer. I turned and left before he had time to give it further thought.

I was surprised that his attorney did not contact me with some kind of settlement offer. I found out why at the trial held before a judge. He didn't have representation. He defended himself, and, of course, he lost. I put Mrs. Thornton on the stand, and the second mechanic testified. The defendant put himself on the stand to state that he did an overhaul of the existing transmission and claimed $3,000 was his charge for doing an overhaul. He said that he never promised her a new transmission. Of course, I reminded him that perjury was a crime. I was not anywhere as near intimidated when he was in the courtroom as when I served him with a summons. In fact, on the stand, he didn't look so imposing, not nearly so big as he looked back in the valve manufacturer's office.

The judge ruled in our favor and ordered the defendant to pay Mrs. Thornton $3,000, some of which should have been mine except for one little fact that I left out. Mrs. Thornton was Barbara's aunt. My wife had asked me to do this one for free because poor Mrs. Thornton didn't have the money to pay me. Anyway, practice makes perfect, I thought.

A few days later, I received a letter from someone who selected my name at random from a list of young lawyers published by the bar association. The letter was from an inmate at Elmira State Hospital, a maximum-security hospital for the criminally insane. Here's what it said:

Dear Sir:

My name is Norman Brown. I am seventy-two years old and I am in a state-run hospital for the criminally mentally ill. I have been an inmate of this prison for fifty years. When I was twenty-one, I was charged with killing my wife. We had been married for only six months, but I drank an awful lot during those days. I was charged with manslaughter. They said that I struck her in a drunken rage. I guess that she hit something when she went down. I have no memory of doing that. I was found not guilty, however, because they said I was insane, so they committed me to this place. As I said, that was fifty years ago. I don't want to be free. I have no family and no place to go. But I would like to go to a place to live out my life that is not so harsh. I don't belong here. Can you help me?

Hoping that you are a caring person, I am yours,

Norman Brown

Immediately, I went to the statute. What I found was this: If someone is found not guilty of a violent crime by reason of insanity, that person shall be committed to an institution for the criminally insane until sane. Until sane! I couldn't believe what I was reading. It meant that this man would probably have received a prison sentence of ten or 12 years if he had been found guilty of manslaughter. Because he was determined to be insane, however, he was in his 50th year of imprisonment because doctors and administrators determined that he was still insane.

I believe that many lawyers receiving this letter would have not responded or would have turned down the plea for help by citing a busy practice as an excuse. I decided at least to investigate. After all, I wasn't the busiest lawyer in town. I thought that a visit to Mr. Brown would be in order.

When I arrived at the facility it didn't surprise me that I had to show my ID and proof that I was an attorney. I was a bit surprised that I had to walk through a screening device and through doors that had to be unlocked for me to enter. Then, with guards on either side of me, I walked through an open area containing a small group of inmates.

"Sit!" one of the guards shouted. The prisoners complied. We then walked past a string of small cells inhabited apparently by only one person per cell. Some of these prisoners were quite vocal as we passed, extending their arms through the bars and shouting meaningless words and phrases, jabberwocky.

Finally, we arrived at a conference or interview room. It was empty.

"The prisoner will be brought in," one of the guards said. "Do you want a guard in the room with you?"

"Not unless you think it's dangerous for me to be alone with him."

"Naw," the guard said. "He's a harmless old man."

Just then, Norman Brown was brought into the room.

"He's all yours," said the guard.

"I'm Tony Boudreau," I said, introducing myself. "You wrote me a letter."

"Thank you for coming, Mr. Boudreau," he said. I was relieved to hear his polite, normal response. I had had some trepidation about how the man would behave. I couldn't help but study his manner and his appearance. He looked considerably older than his 72 years. His facial skin was wrinkled and leather-like, probably from his days in the yard, a privilege, I learned later, given to all prisoners who were not considered dangerous and behaved well. Surprisingly, he had a full head of hair albeit totally grey. He held himself in a slightly stooped posture as though he had a great weight on his shoulders. After our initial greeting, he sat heavily on one of the two straight, wooden chairs placed on either side of a small conference table. I sat across from him.

"I read your letter," I said, "and did a little research. I'm not certain that I can help you, but I'm willing to try. The law says that you have to stay here until you are sane. Do you feel that you're sane?"

"I'm very old," he said.

"Yes, but do you feel that you are now a sane person?"

"I've been here a long time," he responded.

Suddenly, I realized that communication might not be as simple as I hoped. "Do you remember the letter you sent me?" I asked.

"Can you help me? They say that I'm mentally ill. Nuts, I guess."

"Do you remember the letter?"

"Yes, I sent you a letter to see if you could help me."

"I read your letter," I said. "Do you feel that you are sane after all this time?"

"I don't know. Here everyone … acts out all the time. I try to stay out of trouble best I can."

He repeated what he had said in the letter but disjointedly, making it obvious to me that he had some help with writing the letter, maybe a guard or some kind of prison counselor.

"Do you get some psychiatric care" I asked.

"There's a doctor. I guess he's a psychiatrist or psychologist or something like that. They call him the shrink. Mostly, he deals with the inmates that make trouble. I never make trouble."

"You said that you wanted to live the rest of your life somewhere else. What did you have in mind?"

"I heard that there are hospitals that treat people like human beings. I understand that they even give you some kind of treatment to make you better. I'd like to go to one of those places."

A little claustrophobia set in about then, so I became anxious to wrap it up.

"Look," I said, "I'll see what I can do." I shook his hand and got out of there.

Frankly, I didn't know where to start. I thought about giving Spike a call, but I had to stand on my own two feet, flat as they were. I toyed with the habeas corpus concept, the Constitutional right to have the body produced, in this case a live one tucked away in a facility that I felt was not appropriate for this "harmless old man," as the guard described him. However, I thought that habeas corpus was a little far-fetched. But the answer was really obvious: The law was the problem, so change the law. But how?

I met the problem head-on. Who creates laws? Legislatures create laws, so I made an appointment to see my local legislator.

To my amazement, he was perfectly receptive to helping me change the law. A short discussion resulted in our agreeing that if someone was found not guilty of a crime by reason of insanity but was determined to be not dangerous to himself or others and was incarcerated in a hospital for the criminally mentally ill, that person could be transferred to a hospital for the mentally ill upon application to the administrator of the hospital for the criminally mentally ill. If that sounds like a good deal of jargon, that's exactly what it was. However, it also sounded exactly like most legislation. In any case, he introduced the bill saying that or something to that effect.

I watched with some fascination as the bill breezed through committee and went to the floor where it passed without a whimper. Shortly thereafter, my legislator notified me that the governor had signed the bill, enacting it into law. Hardly anyone, including the governor, paid much attention to the bill's content apparently. What a system! Not only that, but the legislator presented me with the pen used by the governor to sign the bill into law.

Upon formal application from me as counsel to Norman Brown, he was transferred to the State mental hospital in Poughkeepsie, a much more pleasant place than the hospital for the criminally mentally ill. Not only that, some real psychiatrists were there to provide treatment. Once again, the money did not flow in, but I had accomplished some good, and I was learning to become a reasonably good lawyer. It turned out, however, that I was not the most popular lawyer when it came to mentally ill facilities administrators. In the following six months, 88 inmates applied for a transfer, causing general mayhem for busy administrators and clerks.

FRANK AT 27

From the time I was seventeen, I wanted to make the Army my career. It was the life for me – structure, organization, discipline, opportunity for advancement, and, as the foot soldiers say, "three squares a day." That's why it was so disappointing, so frustrating now to be denied that career. The Army and the Veteran's Administration were going to take care of me, but I could no longer serve. I was honorably discharged with retirement pay and a spate of medals with the added benefit of health care for the rest of my life. I would need that health care. My head continued to throb for weeks at a time, my body was generally racked, and I couldn't hear worth a damn in my left ear. Even worse, the pain that started with morphine and similar drugs in the Army continued with a variety of drugs purchased after I left the Army. Then, when I was told that I had to cut back on those, I looked elsewhere for help. Alcohol helped some also, and that's how I spent more and more of my time drinking in a bar called Teddy's. It was there that I met Sally.

She was tall and thin with flowing blonde hair and had a penchant for ridiculing guys who approached her. She was at Teddy's every Friday night for Karaoke. Her performances were something to behold. She could sing songs that had the joint rocking and she could croon a tune that would melt your heart. I was deeply in love with her before we ever exchanged a word.

I was stunned when she approached me.

"Hey, it's your turn," she said. "You're up."

At first, I thought surely she was talking to someone behind me.

"Are you talking to me?" I asked, then repeated just in case she didn't hear: "Are you talking to me?"

"Who are you, Robert De Niro?"

Then, she did an amazing De Niro imitation in her lowest possible female base voice: "Are you talking to me?"

I laughed. It was very funny, I thought.

"No," I said, "I'm no De Niro. My name is Frank, Frank Foley … and I don't sing, not in public anyway."

She sized me up. "I see you sitting here by yourself very Friday night. Don't you like people?"

"You can sit and talk to me if you want – between songs, I mean, or when you're bored with your friends."

She virtually floated to the chair next to me and stuck out her hand. "Sally, Sally Withers."

Grasping her hand was immediately remedial. The soft, tender hand magically soothed the aches in my body. Even better, she reached over with her left hand and cupped my fist. Double pleasure.

"So, you enjoy listening to amateurs embarrass themselves?" she asked.

"I've enjoyed the singing, all of it, but you … you're very good," I answered her.

"Look," she said, "Is there something you don't like about me? I see you here every week and not once have you hit on me."

"I, ah, just enjoy the music – and the alcohol, I guess."

"Does that make you happy?"

"It's a long story," I answered.

"I'm available. Let's hear it."

"No, not tonight," I said. "Maybe some time."

"Next Friday night?"

"You are persistent, aren't you? ... Maybe."

"I'll tell you what," she said. "Next Friday, we'll quit early, and you can buy me a cup of coffee. Can you handle that?"

"Absolutely," I answered.

The following Friday was the beginning of a number of Friday nights of coffee and much more. I have no idea what she saw in me. I wasn't the best-looking guy around with my war-torn face. She didn't seem to notice, never even commented on it when we became much closer. I was relaxed and happy, except for the damn headaches. Finally, I told her about those and how only alcohol and some prescription drugs – taken together – seem to ease the pain for a while. Then one night, she suggested a new remedy.

"I have a friend," she began, "who might be able to help, but you should know the worst about him. He pushed illegal drugs when he was a teenager and he spent some time in prison, but that's all behind him. He still knows a whole lot about all kinds of drugs. He might be able to help you if the doctors aren't doing it for you."

"You mean take illegal drugs like marijuana?"

"There are all kinds of drugs," Sally said, "even different kinds of marijuana. Some of them are even legal because the laws just can't define them. Do you want me to talk to him for you?"

"I don't know," I said. "The VA has been helpful, but the stuff they're giving me is just not doing the job. Yeah, sure, talk to him if you really think he can help and he's not just peddling again."

"I'm sure that he's not selling illegal drugs. The fact is that he's a really smart guy and a remarkable researcher. If anyone can find a drug that's helpful and not technically illegal, he's the guy."

"All right," I said. "Talk to him."

Sally's friend did indeed find a form of drug that was not defined in the statutes as an illegal drug. Much to my surprise, it helped enormously. Deep into the night when the pain was at its worst, the drug relaxed me completely, and the pain disappeared. For the first time, I thought that some drugs were not available in drug stores and still were legal drugs. But there was a significant downside. I needed to use more and more of the stuff, it seemed, to reach that necessary level.

Then, I met Sally at Roxy's on a Friday night that would be the most horrible night of my life. Not only was I accelerating the use of the undefined drug, but I was losing touch with reality. I thought that Sally was especially beautiful that night, and she sang magnificently. But I was in a virtual stupor. I remember leaving the club with her, but that was my last memory for a number of hours.

Sometime during the night, I had passed out. When I awoke, I was in a strange surrounding. I was laying face down in a hard patch of uncared for grass. My entire body ached as though I had fallen hard to the ground or maybe even thrown there. A large oak tree loomed over me. I peered around once and saw no one. Then I realized that it was an alley way behind a row of businesses closed for the day and bars closed for the night. To my surprise, I still had money in my pocket and my watch was still on my wrist, thus dispelling my first thought that I had been mugged and then dumped in the alley. The watch told me that it was 4:10 a.m., still quite dark in the alley without light save for that provided by a half-moon.

Slowly, I picked up my stiff, sore body and stood taking in the setting. Even though it was evident that I was to the rear of restaurants and bars, I didn't recognize exactly which ones. I was quite lost. I could hear distant sounds of traffic, so I moved in that direction. I stumbled and slammed against a dumpster that I hadn't noticed before. The cover was flipped over and, suddenly, I saw a gruesome sight. A woman's body lay upon the heaps of bottles, cans, newspapers, and other miscellaneous garbage. The woman laid face down with her head tilted in an unorthodox angle from her shoulders. Everything below her waist was submerged in the dumpster's content, but then I saw just a part of her ripped, splattered blouse. A massive kick in the pit of my stomach told me that the blouse was Sally's.

I fell to my knees and lost the contents of my stomach. Suddenly the alley was flooded by the headlights of a patrolling police car. The officer lowered his window.

"Are you all right, fella?"

I wasn't remotely all right.

"No, I need your help." That's all I could say. I pointed toward the opening of the dumpster.

He exited the police car. "Just sit there a minute," he ordered, "while I see what's going on."

When he looked into the dumpster, he flinched. "What the hell?"

"I … I just found her there," I stammered.

"I'm cuffing you and then I'm going to get some people out here. What the hell?" he said again.

After he called headquarters, we sat in his car for a few minutes.

"Look," he said, finally. "You can tell me what happened here if you want, but I'll tell you right now that you have a right to remain silent and anything you say can be held against you in a court of law."

"I can't tell you anything," I said, "because I don't know anything. I know that girl in there, but I have no idea what happened."

"OK, let's have the professionals talk to you. Why don't you just sit there until they give me the green light to take you in. Maybe you should start thinking a little harder about what happened."

When the homicide detective and other police arrived, they examined the dumpster and the area around it for a while, then a detective opened the door of the squad car where I sat cuffed.

"What's your name?"

"Frank Foley," I answered.

"OK, Mr. Foley, we're going to have the officer take you to police headquarters while we deal with the body here. We're going to talk to you there and give you an opportunity to contact a lawyer."

The twenty-minute ride to the police station was a blur. I still felt generally banged up and now the headache was returning. When we arrived, they removed the handcuffs and put me in a questioning room.

"Do you need a doctor?" one of the detectives asked.

"I don't think so, but I think that I hit the ground pretty hard."

"We're going to ask you some questions. If you think that you need a lawyer, we'll let you make a call, but if you're not responsible for that body in the dumpster, you'll probably want to go ahead and answer our questions."

Even though I had no memory of what happened from the time I left the club to the time I regained consciousness on the grass next to the dumpster, I was certain that I had not been responsible for such a terrible thing. My God, it was Sally. I could not have hurt her.

"I don't know if I can help, but I don't need a lawyer. I'll answer whatever questions I can."

Detective Andrew Mallory was a seasoned investigator. He came from a family of police officers so he never had a thought of pursuing any other profession. He wasn't on the beat very long before his supervisors saw that this was a thorough, efficient, tough cop who would make Detective very rapidly. Now, he had held that job for a dozen years because he was good at it. He sat in a chair across the conference table from me. I took one look at him and knew that I was in for a bumpy ride. Of course, other police officers were viewing the questioning through a one-way glass, and of course they heard every word through the small concealed sound system.

"Okay, Mr. Foley, let's clear up some mysteries. We're going to identify the body pretty quickly, but you can do that for us, can't you?"

"She was a friend, a good friend. Her name is Sally Withers, at least that's who I think I saw there in the heap of garbage. I didn't see her face when I looked into the dumpster, but I was with her earlier in the evening. I recognized her blouse and her hair. It was so horrible. I looked at her for only a second, but I knew it was Sally."

Clearly, it was not Detective Mallory's practice to pepper a suspect with questions. He calmly waited until I finished talking. Finally, he asked a direct question: "Did you kill her, Frank?"

"I don't know who did such a terrible thing," I said, "but I wouldn't have done anything that would have harmed her in any way. She was a wonderful person."

Mallory looked me over. "You're going to have to explain exactly how you happened to be found near a dumpster containing a body, a woman that you know. Unless you have a plausible explanation, we're going to have to charge you with murder, Frank."

"That's the thing," I said. "I don't know what happened from the time I left the club until the time I woke up near the dumpster."

Of course, Detective Mallory didn't believe that. I could hardly blame him. He put me under formal arrest and charged me with murder. The next morning, I was arraigned and given my rights by a judge who looked already convinced of my guilt.

That was just the beginning of a long, difficult period in my life. I could not obtain bail because of the seriousness of the charge, my head was throbbing with new intensity, and I was no longer in the position of obtaining the only drugs that had provided some relief.

Naturally, I called on the friend who had rescued me from minor scrapes and inconveniences, Spike Dumbrowski. Within an hour, Spike was in the cell with me.

"I'm going to help you," Spike said. "There's no way in hell that you were capable of killing that woman. You just wouldn't do that. I've known you too long to believe that you're guilty of this terrible crime."

"Wait a minute," I said. "You can't help me directly; you're a First Assistant State's Attorney in another county, but you can get me some representation, right?"

"No, Frank, I'm going to do it myself. Look, I've been thinking about leaving the State's Attorney's Office for a while. I always thought I'd rather go over to the other side, do defense work in my own firm."

"You're going to do that now, for me?"

"You bet. Hey, for myself, too. I'm not making any sacrifices. And I've already got a partner planned. Of course, I'm going to bring in …"

"Tony! Yeah!"

"All right, buddy," Spike said. "I'll be back tomorrow as a defense attorney after I resign this afternoon. We're going to probe deep and see what went down here."

SPIKE AT 28

I loved my job as a prosecutor. Putting the bad guys away felt just right. But here I was, young, bright, and ambitious. All around me, I was being told that I would surely be the State's Attorney some day, maybe even a judge. In law school, however, I saw myself as a future – dare I say it? – Perry Mason. That's right. I wanted to be the lawyer who defended the innocent guy who was charged with a villainous crime. Yes, the innocent guy. Not only that, like Perry, I would zoom in on the real criminal. So it wasn't rocket science to make the decision. I wanted my own defense firm, and Frank needed me now.

"Frank," I said, seeing him in his county jail cell the next day, "I need you to tell me everything you know, not only about that night but from the time you first met Sally."

Sure, I listened politely when he told me the Karaoke meeting story, and I was devastated that he had been in all that agony when I wasn't there to help, but I didn't really get excited until he told me about the drugs.

"Who is this guy?" I asked. "Him, I want to hear about."

"I completely trusted Sally," Frank said. "She told me that he was legit, that he wasn't dealing in illegal drugs, and that he could help me."

"When did you last see him?"

"Spike, I'm an idiot," Frank said. "I never even met him. Sally said that would be best. It would protect us both."

"All right," I said, "tell me this: Are you certain that the drugs weren't illegal?"

"I trusted her and I guess she trusted him. Look, the VA stuff wasn't touching my pain. This stuff, whatever it was, helped."

"We'll find him," I said. "We have to find him, because he has some explaining to do."

"Spike, how is this going to help us?" Frank asked. "Do you think that he could have killed Sally?"

"That's a possibility, of course," I said, "but right now I want to get that drug to a lab. You have some, don't you?"

"Just a remnant. It's hidden in my apartment. Sally would get it for me only when I asked her to. She said it was too dangerous for me to have around. She said she would get it for me only when I needed it. ... Spike?"

"Yes, buddy, what?"

"I don't know what that drug did to me. I can't believe I would have hurt her, but how can I know?"

"I know," I said. "I know you, Frank. You're not capable of such a thing. You couldn't take a life like that."

"But I did, Spike, I mean take a life. I killed in Vietnam. I took human lives. How can I know I didn't do that again without realizing that I did?"

"Look," I said. "I know that wars change people and I know that drugs can greatly influence how someone thinks and acts, but we're going to assume that you could not have done this. Now it's our job to find out who did this terrible thing. We'll stay in close touch with the police, but our private investigators will be examining the thing in fine detail. Our friend Tony's involved, too, in our investigation. Neither Tony nor I will let you down." All the while, however, I was thinking, *how on earth can I find a way to help Tony. Was I up to the task?*

That was more bravado than sincere belief when I reassured Frank. It sure didn't look good for him – he was using drugs, he

107

had no memory of his actions, and he was found in the close vicinity of the murdered victim. Nevertheless, I just couldn't believe that Frank was guilty.

Our obvious first objective was to find the mystery drug provider. While continuing to pepper the police about their progress, Tony led two investigators we had recently hired to assist us. Both had been with the Illinois State Police, one a veteran investigator and the other an experienced lab technician.

Mike saw many drugs pass through the State Police lab in connection with a variety of crimes, so when we were able to get the remnant from Frank's apartment, Mike was able to identify it. "This one," he said, "is rare, but I've seen it. It's the only one I know that would completely blast out memory for a prolonged period. And it's perfectly legal."

"Isn't it marijuana?" Tony asked.

"A form of marijuana. As far as I can tell, it's Spice, legal herbs laced with synthetic cannabis. The herbal extracts are made up of Blue Lotus flowers, Bay Bean. Decamf Skillings, Lion's Tail, and others, all legal."

"This sounds stupid," I said, "but I didn't know it was marijuana. It was helping."

"It could relieve some pain," Mike explained, "but at high doses, users may feel like their body is merging with an inanimate object or that they are traveling through time. At overdose levels, panic attacks, coma, memory loss, and schizophrenia can occur."

"And that's why," Tony said, "Frank may have been comatose during a period and why he suffered memory loss."

"Okay," I said. "Now we know that this drug may have rendered Frank incapable of committing the crime, but I'm concerned about the panic attack and schizophrenia aspects, personality disorders that often initiate criminal behavior. ...

Tony, let's get permission to get a complete physical examination of Frank in his cell."

"Physical?" Tony said.

"Yes," I replied. "It's just a hunch. We know what the drug might have done to Frank mentally. I want to see if there are any clues as to what his body has been through."

While we were in the process of setting up the physical, Jerry, our other former State Policeman, was talking to everyone he could find with any association with Roxy's or with Sally Withers. Then he struck gold in the form of Mitch, Roxy's janitor. Mitch thoroughly enjoyed his job. He was there at the 3:00 a.m. closing to mop up and clean up. He worked for a few hours and then he was finished for the day except on those occasions when Roxy wanted him to set up for special group parties in late afternoons. That gave him all the time he needed to watch ball games and soaps. He wasn't terribly ambitious, but he did like attention. So, when Jerry approached him about whether he had seen someone who might be the mystery drug provider, he was more than willing to help.

"Sure, I know exactly who you're talking about," Mitch said, with an air of importance. "I've seen the guy talking to poor Sally just outside the rear exit. He's a real creep type. I even know his name."

"Terrific," Jerry said.

"Look," Mitch said, "is there some kind of reward for this type of information? You know I don't make a whole lot of money here."

"No, no reward, but I do have a fifty-dollar bill in my pocket if that will help."

Mitch's eyes lit up when he was presented with the fifty.

"Good," Mitch said. "They call him Spider. I don't have the full name, but he hangs around the local bars. I know he did some time, but he's stayed clean from what I can tell. The cops don't bother him."

This conversation was reported to me verbatim when Jerry returned to my office. The guy has a digital recorder for a brain.

"What now?" Jerry asked.

"I'd be surprised," I said, "if the police haven't already contacted this Spider guy, but maybe they're so hung up on Frank's involvement with the crime that they haven't looked past their noses. If that's the case, let's find him and see what he has to say."

"Want to come along for the ride?" Jerry asked.

"Why not?" I said. "I can't help Frank sitting around the office."

It wasn't that difficult to locate Spider. Even though he moved surreptitiously and typically met clients in alleys rather than inside of buildings, he boosted about his "legal" activities. We spotted him proceeding into an alley around Midnight and approached him from Jerry's vehicle.

"Hey, Spider, can we talk to you for a minute?" Jerry shouted.

"Do I know you guys?" Spider asked.

"We want to ask you a few questions. We'd like to find out what you know about the death of Sally Withers," Jerry said.

"So you're cops?" Spider said.

"No, we're not," I said. "I'm a lawyer. I represent Frank Foley. This is my investigator."

"I don't need to talk to you guys," the recalcitrant Spider said.

"No, no you don't," I agreed, "but when the police hunt you down, there will be plenty of questions. Your silence now is pointing the finger right at you. The police won't be talking to you in an alley. You'll be in a jail cell."

"I don't know nothing," Spider said.

"We know that you were supplying cannabis to Frank Foley," I said, "and you were doing it through Sally."

"I gave her legal stuff. That's all. I don't know what she did with it. I'm clean. The cops have nothing on me."

Jerry sized him up. "I'm going to ask you a big question, one that the police are going to ask. Where were you from nine o'clock to Midnight the evening of Sally's death?"

"Do I look like some kind of Einstein? How do you expect me to remember where I was every minute of my life? I don't have a clue."

"All right," I said. "We're going to leave you to the police. Maybe they'll convince you that you're Einstein after all. We'll be seeing you in court if not sooner."

Unfortunately, the police had little interest in our friend Spider. Even with my volunteered information, the police were comfortable with the assumption that they had the killer of Sally Withers in custody. After all, he was found within a few feet of a strangled body. Why look further? Quite ridiculously, I thought WWPMD – What Would Perry Mason Do? Naturally, he would not only prove his client not guilty but would somehow trick the real culprit into an open court confession. A bit of a tall order.

Tony was not only an associate of mine now in the practice of law, but he remained a good friend. Then there was the bonus: He had his head on straight while I tended to be carried away with my brilliance. He kept me on target in the State v. Foley.

"They have absolutely no evidence against Frank," Tony said. "He was there, that's all. At most, he's a suspect because of the circumstances. They're holding him while they try to make a connection to prove he's guilty."

"On the other hand," I said, "we have no evidence that he didn't commit the crime. We don't really know what happened."

"Ah, but a good prosecutor like you knows well that he must be found guilty beyond a reasonable doubt. I don't see that happening."

"Maybe we don't fret about it until we complete discovery, until we see what they have. In the meantime, it's clear that

Spider knows much more than he's saying. Let's apply some pressure somehow."

Tony leaned back, his fingers intertwined behind his head, a posture that always demonstrated especially pensive thought. "Let's do this," he said. "Let's catch Spider in that alley and beat the crap out of him."

"Heck of an idea," I said, "but we are lawyers, so that's probably not in our best interest. No, what we need is trickery. We have to make this guy believe we know more than we know. Then, maybe, he may just slip and reveal something that we can use." *Why didn't they have a course in this lawyer trickery stuff in law school?* I thought.

"All right," Tony said. "Let's give him another jolt."

Once again, it wasn't all that difficult to find Spider. We drove the area and stopped to look down each alley. The third stop did it. There he was, oddly lurking outside of a restaurant door. "What does he do in mid-winter," I said. "Surely, he moves in somewhere."

"Hey, Spider," I hollered, "we're ba-a-a-a-ck."

"Well, le-a-a-a-ve," he countered. I didn't think that Spider was that clever.

"I want to talk about a trade," I said. "I have some information you can use in your line of work."

"What are you talking about?" he asked.

"Look," Tony said, "I've spent the last day doing some legal research. I've found six methods of providing mind-expanding drugs that do not contain elements detailed in the statutes that outlaw drugs."

"Why would you share that information with me?"

"A trade," I said. "That's what I'm talking about. We'll trade Tony's research for a little information from you."

"Depends on what you want to know," Spider said.

"We think that Sally was rotten," I told him. "We have reason to believe that she was double-crossing you. You were providing her with the stuff for Frank, but he wasn't getting it. She took advantage of his state of mind. She was parceling the drugs to your other buyers for bigger bucks. We want to know who those buyers were."

"You think one of them is responsible for Sally's death?" Spider asked.

"Sally conned you, Spider, plain and simple," Tony said. "We want to find out which of your customers might be particularly upset by that."

"I'm not giving names. I don't need your stinking information," Spider retorted. "I have all the legal drugs I need."

"We'll find them," I said, "and we might find you right in the middle of this."

"Look," Spider said, "I don't want you hounding my customers and spooking them. I'll give you the names of the two people Sally supplied at the Karaoke bar. That's it. Do I get the legal research?"

"Sure. We need the two names and everything you can tell us about them – home address, background, where they hang out."

Surprisingly, Spider was cooperative for legal research that wasn't all that valuable. Both Tony and I knew that the Legislature was going to close those loopholes; it was just a matter of time.

Our investigation was just one short step ahead of the police. We learned later that Detective Mallory, too, became less convinced of Frank's guilt when Frank's memory slowly returned to the point that now he could tell the police exactly when he lost consciousness. In our next visit to Frank's cell, he reported that he had told the police this: "Sally decided that it was time for me to learn the truth about her. She suggested that we take a leisurely walk so that we could be alone. That's when she told

113

me that she had been working as a contact between other users and Spider. I learned that he had been dealing in drugs that were narrowly legal but demands required him to deal in illegal drugs also. He thought that if he didn't have any direct contact with the users, we could lay it all on Sally if the police caught up with him. His reasoning was stupid, but that's how he figured it. What he didn't know was that Sally was skimming. She was charging more for the stuff than she was giving to Spider. On our walk, she told me that she wanted out before Spider found out what was happening. She never had that opportunity.

From out of nowhere, something hit me. It was a blow to the side of my head that already was scarred by my Vietnam injury, I guess, because that's when it all went dark. I can remember everything up until that time. The next thing I remember is waking up near the dumpster."

We reported our findings to Detective Mallory. Tony and I were impressed with his efficiency. After talking to the users that Spider gave us, the police honed in on Spider's over-all activities. In short, Spider was arrested for drug peddling, a charge that would send him back to prison for a long time. This led to a deal and a confession of the killing of Sally Withers. He claimed that he didn't mean to kill her, that it was not premeditated. He just wanted to "rough her up a little bit, teach her a lesson." The deal called for avoiding the death penalty and dropping the drug charges. He said that he had stepped out of the shadows behind Frank and struck him with an old-fashioned blackjack. All he wanted to do, he said, was teach Sally a lesson, but he went too far. When he realized he had killed her, he dropped her in the dumpster and left Frank there to take the blame. He pleaded guilty to manslaughter.

Frank, Tony, and I celebrated Frank's release from that jail cell with burgers and shakes at the local Steak 'n Shake.

"You know," Frank said, "My mind is a complete mystery. I thought that I lost it when I was recovering from head wounds in Vietnam, but I was thinking all right when I got home, even though my head still hurt. Then, I thought that I lost it again because of drug use, but it rallied again by giving me recollections I didn't know I had."

"Are you going to make out all right with the pain thing?" Tony asked.

"I think so. As you know, I had to be off everything but proper medications when I was in jail. Those have finally worked for me. Yeah, I think I'm going to be fine."

"We'd like you to come to work with us," I told Frank. "We're the most promising law firm in town. We can use your leadership abilities somewhere."

"Thanks, but I've decided I'd like to teach – history. Uncle Sam is going to pay my tuition so I'm going to get a degree and become a high school teacher."

We were bowled over at first. Then I thought: *Frank will be a great teacher!*

FRANK AT 31

I was so anxious to become a member of the U.S. Army when I graduated from high school that I barely gave college a thought. However, I was able to pick up some college credits while I was in service. It was at least a start, I thought, even though I never could keep up with Spike and Tony who had shaky starts but then managed to become lawyers. But after the Sally-Spider drug debacle, I became a full-time student and was able to get my diploma, a degree in education.

I thought that I would be way out of the picture attending college with 19- to 23-year-olds, but the kids were great. My partying days were over, but I established a wonderful camaraderie with the younger students in the classroom and in the gym. Finishing first in my college class did wonders for my ego and led to my first job as a teacher at Plattsburgh High School in Upstate New York. I taught American History to Juniors and Seniors, and it was a blast. Of course, I had war stories – actual war stories – so that helped to keep their attention. I was fascinated myself how war could be compared and contrasted in how they were fought from the marching in formation into battle of the British in the Revolutionary War to fighting in the cold of Korea and in the bushes of Vietnam.

Perhaps the best day of my life – up to that point – was my first day of teaching. I not only experienced the pleasure of teaching twenty-eight enthusiastic students, but I met Laura. I was waved over to a table in the lunch room by the Physical

Education teacher, Kevin Burns, a jock if I ever saw one. At the table, I was introduced to Max Hilton, a Science teacher, Carrie Smith, a Music teacher, and Laura, the woman who was to become the love of my life.

"Always good to see a new face," Max said. "And the best part is that you're still standing after a morning of teaching high school students."

"If my afternoon students are nearly as uplifting as my morning students," I said, "this will be a remarkable day."

"Good for you," Max said, "May your enthusiasm continue for at least another day."

"Don't pay attention to Max," Carrie said. "He's just a stuffy old Science teacher who thinks that every student should study twelve hours a day."

"Keep those good thoughts," Laura said. "This is your first teaching job?"

"The very first, but I did some teaching in the Army."

"Ah, we have a vet in our midst," Max said.

"Look," Kevin said, "I have some interesting information about Frank just in case he's too modest to tell you himself. He's not only a vet but something of a war hero, so treat him accordingly."

"Kevin," I admonished him, "please don't do that to me. My life is starting here and now. Everything in the past is gone and forgotten. Thanks, anyway, for the buildup."

"I, for one, would like to hear about some of the past," Laura said. "I have a naturally inquiring mind, as everyone here will tell you."

"Sure, anytime," I said.

Laura had eyes that never stopped shining. When she stood, I saw that she was about 5'10, just a few inches shorter than I, but it wasn't her height that immediately attracted me. She was just overwhelmingly beautiful from her blonde, flowing hair to the sparkling eyes to the short, pertly shaped nose to lips that were a delicacy to a chin that was in perfect juxtaposition to her face and neck. I was stunned with her beauty from the very beginning.

"Same time, same place tomorrow?" she asked.

"If he lasts 'till then," Max added.

Kevin gave me the much-needed information – 26 years old, engaged once, but she called it off when she determined that her fiancé's ego was larger than his faithfulness. So, she was single! I almost leapt in joy at the news but became immediately despondent when I honestly assessed my chances. Here I was a guy with a beat-up face, a hearing problem, and a first year's teacher's salary. Hell, I didn't even know if I was going to be any good at this teaching gig.

Laura gave me new hope the next day, though, when she sat next to me at the luncheon table. "Okay," she said, "tell me about the hero stuff, then I'll never ask you again."

"Really, all I did was to lead my company into a battle. I didn't have the sense to stay low, so I got shot up. The Army is big on handing out medals, so they gave me some. It's good publicity for recruiting, you know. Anyway, I'm here to be a hero like you, somebody who helps formulate young minds."

"I'll settle for that answer," Laura said. "Now, when are you going to take me to dinner?"

"What?"

"You heard me. I'm very good at reading minds. If that's not on your mind, tell me."

I was shocked, of course. "Am I that easy to read?" I asked.

"I'm just guessing. Don't worry. I can't really read your innermost thoughts."

"I'm no prize even for a dinner date, but you bet I'd like to take you to dinner. Who wouldn't?"

"Well, when and where?" she said.

Two teachers with a dinner date. I couldn't believe my good fortune. Not only was she amazingly attractive but she had good taste, obviously. Then I remembered Sally and the first time that she approached me in the karaoke bar. Then it struck me – Laura was simply being nice to the new kid. She saw in me what Sally had seen – a rather pathetic figure that needed a friend.

"I guess you're the welcoming committee for new teachers," I said.

I could see that I hurt her.

"Is that what you think, that I ask everyone to take me to dinner? You are guarded, aren't you? Have a good day."

She turned abruptly and left me sitting there, knowing that I had made a major gaffe. As she walked away, I hollered after her. "Laura, wait, please."

She turned and smiled a smile that lit up the room. "Faked you out, didn't I? Well …"

"Sounds wonderful," I said. "Look, I have an Irish name, but in another life, I had to be Italian. Would Pasta House be okay, say at seven?"

"Now you're talking. Do I have to guess which day?"

"You have reduced me to a blabbering idiot in a matter of seconds. Saturday night, this Saturday night, April eighteenth, and I'll pick you up at seven if I get your home address. Did I forget anything?"

"I'll think about it, and if I decide to have dinner with a teacher like you, I'll give you my home address tomorrow, in writing."

"Okay," I said. "It's a deal."

"By the way," she said as she walked away, "never assume anything about me again. That's an order."

I was on a high, but not the kind that I felt when I took questionable medications to reduce pain. No, this was definitely a different feeling, one initiated by a new career and a new friend, at least I was going to do all I could to make her my friend, maybe something much more.

We did have dinner, for me a splendid dinner at a nice Italian restaurant. The food was inconsequential, the ambiance not important, for my mind was enraptured by her very presence. How quickly I had fallen in love. However, what was truly astonishing was that my preoccupation with her presence appeared to be matched by her apparent fascination with me.

"You are so … so contemplative," she said finally after a short silence.

"I'm sorry," I said. "I suppose I've been staring. That's pretty rude. To tell you the truth, I'm not entirely sure whether I had the lasagna or the spaghetti."

"You know that I've been doing a bit of staring myself," she said.

Slowly, she reached across the table and touched the side of my face, two fingers lightly encompassing my damaged ear. "Does it still cause you pain?"

"Once in a while. Paradoxically, that part of my face seems foreign to me. Whenever there's a camera in view, I always turn the right side of my face toward it. How egotistical can I be?"

"You, know, Frank, I never saw any imperfection until you told me about your war experience and put your hand right here." She patted the spot tenderly as she spoke.

As she lifted her luxurious hand from my face, I decided to lighten the moment. "Ah, but beauty is only skin deep. We imperfect people always have that saying to fall upon."

"Enough about you," she said. Let's talk about me. What do you think of my delicate skin? I'm looking for compliments here."

"No apparent defects," I countered. "Do I know you or the superficial you?"

"What you see is what you get."

120

"Get?"

"Don't get carried away. I like you, Frank. I'd like to have you as a friend. I need a good friend. Can you accommodate me?"

"I would consider it a great honor to be your friend. Please feel free to lay your troubles on me."

"And my accomplishments. Can I tell you about those?"

"Sure."

"Okay, good. Accomplishments later but here's a problem. I have a student with a … crush on me. He's become very aggressive, hangs around after class making small talk. He has started to bring me gifts. He says they're small things that he happens to see … had my name on them, perfect for only me."

"Wow! Can't you just say that you can't accept the gifts, that it wouldn't be appropriate for you to take them?"

"I did try that. He's very persistent."

"Has he made any personally aggressive moves; I mean has he tried to touch you in any way?"

"Yes. He's getting a little bolder, touching my arm as he talks to me under the pretense of holding my attention. I'm wondering if there isn't already a buzz around school about a relationship. He may be telling tall tales. I'm getting some odd looks from some of the other students."

"Has he asked personal questions such as whether you were in a relationship?"

"No, but I have a feeling that he's investigated that thoroughly and has determined that I'm single and uncommitted. With student gossip about teachers all the time, no teacher has much of a private life."

"Look," I said, "who am I to cause a heartbreak, but suppose that he discerned – or at least thought that he discerned – that you did have a serious relationship with someone. Wouldn't that chase him off?"

"Do I hear you offering yourself up for the assignment?"

"Of course. Can your reputation and your ego take a hit like that?"

"I have to think about this," Laura said. "It would mean not only convincing him, but it would have to be general knowledge. Do we want that?"

"It would do wonders for my ego," I said.

"Okay, I've thought about it. Let's do it …how?"

"It will require a public show of affection," I said. "You know what? The more I think about it, the more I like this idea."

"Wait a minute!" she said. "This is not a frying pan into the fire kind of thing, is it?"

"Fire, huh? So you think I'm pretty hot?"

"Cool off, temporary lover. Let's figure out how we're going to do this with the least embarrassment to both of us."

I hadn't done much acting, but I understood the role I was about to play. And I had easy motivation. After some deliberation, we developed a plan. Here's how that plan was executed: First, Laura asked her student admirer to stop by fifteen minutes after class to discuss one of the gifts he had left on her desk despite her orders that she really didn't want him to leave the gifts. We knew that he would be right on time for the meeting. As he entered the classroom, he didn't like what he saw. Laura and I were in a close embrace. She was whispering softly in my ear.

"Oh, Billy," Laura said to the surprised student, "Sorry, but you caught us in a tender moment. Do you know my fiancé, Mr. Foley?"

I've seen grief stricken, saddened faces, but Billy topped them all. Of course, he was shaken; the woman of his dreams just announced that she was going to marry another man, really a man, not a teenager.

"I … I didn't know," the stricken student said. "Ahh, do you want me to come back?"

122

"That won't be necessary until you come back for class," I said, seizing the moment. "And, Billy, no more presents."

After Billy left the classroom, my first thought was to congratulate us both for superb acting, but the fact is that we actually felt sorry for Billy.

"Don't feel too bad about it, Laura," I said. "He's young. He'll probably have his heart broken many more times."

"I suppose so," Laura said, "but now what do we do if our little lie goes public?"

"Laugh it off, I suppose," I said. "After all, who would seriously believe that I would have any interest in you. You're much too young and much too beautiful for me."

"Flattery will not get you everywhere, Buddy. I'll tell you what – let's go see a 3D movie tonight; I really don't look so beautiful in those cardboard glasses. That should cool you off."

"Do friends hold hands in the movies?"

"We'll see," Laura said.

* * *

Although they were both very busy with their new law practice, both Spike and Tony kept in touch, inquiring about my new career. Tony called me the evening of the fake engagement.

"How's it going, buddy? Are you one heck of a teacher or what?"

"Could be. I'll have to wait for teacher evaluations but could be, could be," I responded.

"I bet there are no discipline problems. Those kids know that you're a hardened veteran of the wars, right?"

"I think the word's out," I said. "At least they can tell just by looking at me that I've been through some kind of war."

"Come on. You're a whole lot better looking than when you were a squeaky little kid causing trouble."

"Maybe. The jury's still out. Speaking of juries, how's business?"

"Spike and I are enjoying being in practice together. Spike, as always, is brilliant. He puts up with me."

"I have a feeling that you both chose the right profession. Criminal defense mostly?"

"Mostly, but it's odd how a law practice develops. We've done some civil cases also, representing plaintiffs. Actually, that's where the money is, of course. Defending accused criminals is fun, but most criminals don't have money; that's the reason why they're criminals. Nevertheless, if the client who is charged with a crime is indeed innocent, getting that not guilty jury decision is best of all."

"How's your lovely wife?" I asked Tony.

"She's still lovely but a little restless. It seems that she thinks I spend too much time at the office and not enough time at home. We're getting along fine, but there may be trouble on the horizon."

"Maybe you should head those problems off at the pass," I said. "Take the time for flowers, dinner, and a movie occasionally."

"Aren't you the romantic," Tony said. "Maybe you're right and maybe you should give Dear Abby a hand with her column. Enough of that. How about you? You're hanging in on bachelorhood, right?"

"Sure," I said. "I do have a good friend who happens to be quite attractive, but I'm guessing that's where our relationship will stay. I've caused enough trouble with the Sally tragedy to last me a lifetime. Besides, that's how she wants it. Friends only."

"I think Romeo and Juliet started that way," Tony said. "Keep me posted," he said as he hung up.

TONY AT 30

My phone conversation with old pal Frank instigated a change of thinking on my part. I hadn't really voiced Barbara's feelings until it just manifested itself as I talked to Frank. I knew that there was growing dissatisfaction by Barbara because of the time and effort I was putting into the practice. On the other hand, I felt that she should understand that the attention I was giving to the practice was necessary. Other lawyers' wives seem to understand that. Doctors' wives seem to accept the long hours that their husbands would be busy; they find meaningful lives not totally based on the presence of their husbands. Couldn't Barbara do that, at least for the immediate future? Maybe later, I thought, when we have had a successful practice, maybe had associates, perhaps then I could take more time for social engagements, vacations, the niceties of life.

"It's Friday night, for Pete's sake," Barbara said as I walked in the door. "We were supposed to be at the Jacksons an hour ago. Where have you been?"

"Sorry, I didn't realize it was getting that late. I was totally absorbed in a brief I'm preparing."

"You could have called, you know. That would have helped some. At least I would have known that I didn't have to rush myself."

"Again," I said, "I lost track of time."

"Do you still want to go?" she asked.

"Not really," I said. "I'm kind of beat."

"All right. I guess they won't miss us all that much. She's having, I don't know, ten or eleven couples over for outdoor barbeque."

"I'm not a big fan of barbeque. Let's just skip it."

"Okay, Tony," Barbara said. "To tell you the truth, I'm a little wary of the Jacksons. I can't believe the way they snap at each other all the time. They don't care if anyone else is around. You would think that they would at least wait until they're alone to behave like that."

"They're not serious with all that stuff," I said. "Harry is a great teaser. Jennifer gives as much as she gets, it seems to me."

"There's a difference between teasing and cruelty, I think. Harry doesn't use any common sense."

"So I'm late and so we're not going, and so I've saved us from all of that," I said.

"So you think you're a hero. The trouble is that we would have seen other friends there... Shouldn't you and Spike be hiring some associates? I thought that young associates did all the real work for law firms and that the partners got all the credit. Isn't that how it usually works?"

"Maybe we'll get to that point some day," I said, "not in the immediate future, however."

"All right, Tony," Barbara said, "I'll just hang around the house in my robe and slippers hoping to get pregnant. Who needs a social life?"

"Oh, oh, you said the magic word, pregnant. That's going to happen. There's no rush, is there?"

"I suppose not. I hope that we're not still having this conversation ten years from now. Then, it might be too late."

"Barbara," I said, "We agreed that we would have a family when we were both ready. Right now, I don't think we're ready."

"I could go back to teaching, I suppose," Barbara said.

"Do you want to teach?"

"I don't know," she sighed. "I would probably have to get some continuing education hours, get re-certified, and then find an opening. That last part might be the toughest part of all. They're not hiring, except for your friend Frank right out of college."

"I think he's a special case with his Army experience. He can teach about recent history because he lived it."

Barbara frowned. She didn't want to say it, but I know that she was convinced that Frank was hired because people felt sorry for him, first the war experiences and then the false accusations concerning Sally.

"It seems to me," I said, "that you are plenty busy without taking a teaching job with your church activities. When do you have time to miss me anyway?"

"When? Oh, the times you don't make it home to dinner, your early starts to the office, the hours you are in your den preparing for a case or re-working another brief. All those times."

"Peace," I said "We're going to get there. Spike had a big jump; I need to catch up. Having some time for ourselves and to think about Tony, Jr. is coming soon. I promise."

* * *

I thought it was time to discuss the future of the firm with the firm's founder, Spike Dumbrowski. I certainly couldn't find fault with his work ethic. He was a human dynamo, and it wasn't easy keeping up with him. The firm developed very nicely first with our criminal work and then with our civil cases. But there were two monetary problems: the criminal work was successful but fees were minimal (we had no mafia clients) and the plaintiff cases were expensive; we didn't collect until we completed a case and only if we were successful. And the process was long. We were looking at years passing from the time the client walked through the door to the time we would receive a fee for settling or winning at trial. While Spike somehow handled the financing of these endeavors, there wasn't much room for hefty withdrawals for the two partners. What we really needed at this point was some civil work that we could settle quickly, mostly smaller matters paid off by fat insurance companies. With Spike's experience in the State's Attorney's office, some criminal law work wouldn't be bad either if only we had a criminal with money for a change. That's when Harry Jackson walked in the door.

I was surprised to hear from the receptionist that a Mr. Harry Jackson wanted to see me.

"Sure," I told her, "send him right in."

Harry was a big guy, not only in depth but in length. He stood at above six-four and weighed a hefty 280 or so, but he was a jolly type, fuzzy big bear kind of guy. This day, as he entered my office, he was not so jolly.

"Thanks for seeing me, Tony," he said. "I need your help. I think I'm about to get arrested for murder."

"Murder?"

"Jennifer's ... gone. I don't know what happened. Suddenly, she just ... died."

"God, I'm sorry, Harry, but what's all this about murder? And people don't just die. What happened exactly?"

"I'm not sure," Harry said. "She was sniping at me for never being home. You know that feeling, right? I'm busy most of the time. I know you are, so you've probably had conversations like this with your wife."

"I guess I have," I answered, knowing full well that Barbara and I had that discussion just a short time ago.

"Anyway," Harry said, "She was giving it to me with both barrels. I don't know what she expects from me, I mean expected from me. I have a company to run. It's not a nine to five job."

Just then, Spike walked in to my office.

"Oh sorry, I didn't know you were busy," he said.

"No, stay, I want you to hear this. Harry, this is my partner, Spike Dumbrowski. He might as well hear this. Spike, this is Harry Jackson. He lost his wife this morning – I don't know the details yet – but he thinks he's going to be charged with her death."

"I'm sorry to hear about your wife," Spike said, "but would you mind starting from the beginning?"

"Yeah, sure," Harry said. "As I was telling Tony here, I'm a really busy guy. I run a chemical fertilizer business that's booming, so I spend a lot of time at the office. Jennifer, my wife, has been on me because I don't spend enough time at home, but when I am home, she's always having people in. I guess you'd say that she always enjoyed entertaining. We have a mammoth home, and she liked showing it off. Tony and Barbara have been at our home a number of times. Right, Tony?"

I nodded, then said: "Tell us what happened, Harry."

"Right. Well, as I said, she was hassling me because I didn't make it home until really late last night, but I usually can deal with that. I'm a good kidder, so I never take it seriously; sometimes I can just change her mood just like that." He demonstrated the just like that with a snap of his fingers. "This time, though, she just wouldn't let up, so I tried something silly to cheer her up. I tickled her."

"You tickled her?" I said.

"Yeah, you know just to get her going a bit. I reached over and started rubbing my fingers along her back and ribs. She's very ticklish."

"Did that get the result you wanted?" Spike asked.

"I thought so at first. She was screaming for me to stop, but you know I just kind of got into it. I wasn't hurting her, just tickling her."

"Did she fight you off?" I asked.

"Kind of. She was swinging her arms at me, but I just kept it up. Once I got into it, I guess I wanted to teach her a lesson, give her something to remember next time she wanted to complain again about the working thing. I didn't understand her complaints. She had a pretty good life because of all my work."

"Okay, then what happened?" Spike asked. "Did she fall, have a heart attack, a seizure? What happened?"

"None of those things," Harry said. "All of a sudden, she got kind of stiff. All of a sudden, she was on the floor."

"Was she conscious, there on the floor after she collapsed?" I asked.

"No, that's it. She didn't move. I grabbed my cell phone and called 911. I could tell that she wasn't breathing, but I thought that the emergency team could do something. I just didn't know what to do. I never learned CPR or anything like that."

"So when the emergency guys arrived, they told you it was over?" Spike asked.

"Yeah. As soon as they took her out in the ambulance, I left the house. I couldn't stay there any longer. I went to Joe's Bar. I had to have a couple of drinks."

"Why do you think you're going to be arrested?" I asked.

"I got a call on my cell phone from my brother-in-law, Jennifer's brother. He gave me hell for not letting him know. Seems someone at the hospital called him. He never has liked me very much. Then he said that I could bet there would an investigation, that he was going to talk to the police."

"Well, they're not going to arrest you until they have some reasons to suspect foul play," Spike said. "They will want to talk to you, though. I think you should go see them. I'll call and arrange for you to talk to them. If, at any point, they tell you that you're under arrest, stop talking and tell them you want a lawyer, to give you a chance to call me. Okay?"

"Yeah. I'll tell them exactly what happened. I didn't mean to hurt her. This whole thing is so horrible. My Jennifer has died."

"Let me ask you just a few more questions before we call the police," Spike said. "Were you aware that Jennifer had any illnesses, any physical abnormalities?"

"No, no. She was fine as far as I knew."

"She wasn't seeing a doctor for anything?"

"I don't think so. She saw a general physician once in a while, check-ups, colds, things like that."

"I have one question," I said. "Did she have life insurance?"

Harry hesitated before he responded. "Yeah. This isn't going to look too good. We increased our life insurance coverage just last month."

"How much is her policy worth?" I asked.

"That's what's not going to look so good. We increased our policies from $100,000 to a million."

"Was that on the advice of your insurance agent?" I asked.

"In a way. He pointed out to us that term insurance was really cheap at our age, and it wouldn't cost that much to increase the insurance amount, particularly because of my rather large present income."

"Okay," Spike said. "Let's get you down to police headquarters. Just tell them what happened. If the questions begin to get accusatory, stop answering them."

"Aren't you going to come to police headquarters with me?"

"No," Spike said. "That will let them know that you expect to become a suspect. This may be just a routine interview so they can find out what happened. I don't believe that you're suspected of committing any crime at this time. Maybe it will stay that way. Oh, they may want to do an autopsy. Are you willing to allow that?"

"I suppose, if they have to. I don't much like the idea of them cutting up her body like that."

"Look," Spike said, "On second thought, just so they don't think you had a reason for seeing a lawyer, why don't you just go home and wait for a call from the police. If they call, let them know that, of course, you will answer any questions they have about this terrible tragedy."

* * *

The police did call and Harry answered their questions about how the death occurred. He also agreed to an autopsy. It was determined that Jennifer had a rare skeletal disease. Simply, she could not be handled roughly and, in fact, Harry's aggressive tickling was the cause of her death, a truly unbelievable way to die. As it turned out, the police concluded that it was unbelievable. Harry was arrested and charged with the murder of his wife. His phone call was to us, retaining us to defend him.

We visited Harry in his jail cell.

"You'll be arraigned in the morning," Spike said. "You'll be asked to plead guilty or not guilty. Naturally, you'll say not guilty. Then, we'll get down to putting together a defense for you."

"I suppose you want to talk about money, right?"

"Among other things, Harry, yes," I said. "We will represent you if that's what you want." I handed him our fee schedule for representing someone who has been charged with a serious felony.

Having glanced at it, Harry said: "This won't break me, particularly if you guys get me off. As you know, the insurance company owes me a million bucks."

"Not if you're found guilty of murder, Harry," Spike said. "The law does not allow the collection of insurance proceeds if the beneficiary has committed a crime that results in the insurance payment. You know that, don't you?"

"Of course. I didn't mean to hurt her. We were always messing around, giving it to each other. Ask Tony. He's seen the way we went on. Right, Tony?"

"I have indeed, Harry," I answered, "but the prosecution will try to show that you and Jennifer were not getting along, that you increased your insurance because you intended to kill her, and you knew of her condition. Harry, I've seen you arguing with your wife very publicly. Is it true that you wanted to get rid of her?"

"Tony, Tony," he said, "you know that's how we were. We really did get along just fine. Nobody took any of that stuff seriously."

"All right," Spike said, "and the insurance thing was just a fluke. The insurance agent will testify that he approached you about increasing your policies, right?"

"Absolutely."

"Now, here's the big one," Spike said. "We're not going to have the prosecution put a doctor on the stand who will report that you knew all about her unusual condition, right?"

"Never knew that she was fragile."

"We'll want you to tell nothing but the truth if we put you on the stand. Do we have the complete truth from you? Now's the time to tell us the whole truth," Spike said.

"You're going to put me on the stand? You're kidding!"

"Who else can explain your odd relationship?" Spike said. "And who else can testify what you did or did not know? But don't panic yet. Tony and I will want to give this some due consideration."

After we left Harry's cell, we went to the local coffee shop, choosing a table far away from the rest of the recreational coffee drinkers.

"You're not serious about putting him on the stand," I said to Spike.

"Not really, but I want him to tell us everything that he might tell the prosecutor on cross-examination."

"Do you think he's lying to us?"

"Maybe. Murderers lie. I'd like to think that our client's innocent."

* * *

Of course the case went to trial. No way was Harry going to admit that he intentionally killed Jennifer. By trial, we were convinced the death was a terrible accident. It didn't look good, however. Harry's outlandish antics around his wife could be an insurmountable obstacle to overcome with the jury. Spike wanted us both involved in this trial, so I made the opening statement. Spike would close.

The prosecutor, that county's State's Attorney, had experience in felony trials. He went for the jugular in his opening statement. In part, he said: "We're going to demonstrate, through witnesses, how Harry Jackson verbally abused his wife often in public and among friends. We're going to have witnesses tell you that Harry Jackson sought to become a millionaire by purchasing a million-dollar life insurance policy on his wife very shortly before her death, and – most damaging of all - we're going to prove that Harry Jackson's physical abuse of Jennifer Jackson resulted in her death, and that was exactly what he intended."

My opening statement sought to show the jury that Harry was not the villain that the prosecution claimed: "Harry was a kidder, perhaps a somewhat obnoxious one at times, but nevertheless a kidder. He not only teased his wife incessantly, but his reputation for this sort of thing was generally known. While some might consider kidding – teasing – as mean or may be interpreted as bullying, mostly the behavior, for Harry, was much more his method of a friendly relating to others and, of course, especially to his wife. We're going to prove that Harry had no idea that this act of tickling would harm his wife in any way. What's more, Harry was a successful businessman with no need for massive riches; he has done very, very well financially over the years. We will show that the purchase of increased life insurance was based on affordability and the mutual concern Harry and Jennifer had for each other's well-being if either of them should die. Do not let the prosecution fill your minds with mere conjecture. Be certain that the evidence produced by the prosecutor is real evidence, not conjecture. If the prosecutor is not able to produce such evidence, and we know he can't, you must find Harry Jackson not guilty of this terrible charge of murder."

The first witness to be called by the prosecution was Dr. Barton Adrian Hill, an expert in nerve diseases. After establishing the doctor's credentials for the court and the jury, John Denton, the First Assistant State's Attorney, questioned the witness:

"Doctor, is it true that you were requested to assist the coroner in the investigation of Jennifer Jackson's death?"

"Yes, the coroner brought me in because of the unusual circumstances that contributed to her death."

"Did Jennifer Jackson have an identifiable illness that resulted in her death?"

"There was a clear indication that Jennifer suffered from Chronic Inflammatory Demyelinating Polyneuropathy, a condition in which the peripheral nerves become inflamed and damaged."

"What is the cause of the condition?" the prosecutor asked.

The doctor hesitated, trying to find the words that the jury would understand. For the most part, he failed. "It is believed that CIDP, for short, may be caused by an autoimmune reaction in which the body's immune system mistakes the myelin sheath of the peripheral nerves as a dangerous substance and attacks it."

"Would anyone with this condition, such as Jennifer, be aware that she had the problem?" the prosecutor asked.

"She may not have known the exact problem, but clearly she knew she had a problem. I'm certain that she suffered sensations of pain, numbness, pins and needles, tingling."

"So, you're saying that the defendant, Jennifer's husband, had to be aware that unusual, serious activity was occurring in Jennifer's body?"

"Objection," Spike said. "The witness has no knowledge of what the defendant knew, and we have some serious leading going on."

Not surprisingly, the judge agreed with Spike.

"Okay," the prosecutor said, "just let me ask you this: Was Jennifer's symptoms so apparent that anyone could see that she was in pain?"

"Very likely," the doctor said.

When Spike cross-examined the doctor, he concentrated on whether it would have been possible for Jennifer to hide the pain so that Harry was not aware of it. The doctor admitted that Jennifer would have been "an unusual woman indeed not to have shared her discomfiture with her husband, but that it was possible."

The prosecutor then put my neighbor Jim Gleason on the stand. Jim, like the rest of us in the neighborhood, was well aware of Harry's proclivity toward teasing his wife at neighborhood get-togethers. He testified to that effect. Spike had no cross-examination for Jim. Instead, he asked to approach the bench with the prosecutor.

"Your Honor, I see by the witness list that the prosecution has four more neighbors set to testify. Can I ask the prosecutor if he expects all of the others to testify on this point, that Harry was an incurable tease?"

The judge put the question to the State's Attorney and received an affirmative reply.

"We'll concede the point, Your Honor," Spike said, "that the defendant was an insatiable tease along the lines described by the first neighborhood witness. May we pass on the remainder of these say-the-same witnesses?"

"It's all right with me as long as the jury is aware of it," the prosecutor said.

That left just one more witness for the prosecution: insurance agent Herman Mills.

After establishing that Mills was the agent who sold million-dollar policies on Harry and Jennifer, the State's Attorney asked: "Is it true that you made the initial contact with the Jacksons about increasing the insured amounts to a million dollars for each of their lives?"

"No, sir, it is not," Mills replied. "The truth is that Harry brought up the subject when I ran into him at the grocery store."

"What exactly did he say, to the best of your knowledge?"

Mills was slow to answer. "We chatted for a few minutes about how miserable the Bears were this year and then he said something like, you know, I'm wondering how much insurance coverage I would be eligible for. Well, I told him that if he was as healthy as he looked, I could probably get him a million dollars in life insurance if he would be interested."

"Did he say that yes he was interested?"

"Not right away. First, he wanted to know if Jennifer would qualify for a million also. I said, sure, but they both would have to pass physicals. No problem, he said, we're both healthy as can be."

I had no success on cross-examination to give the insurance man's meeting with Harry a different spin. He insisted that it was Harry's initiative totally.

Essentially, that was the case for the prosecution. Now, we had an opportunity to call witnesses for the defense. The prosecution may have been a bit surprised when we called more neighbors to the stand, the very kind of neighbors that were called earlier by the prosecution to report on Harry's mean teasing, a point that we conceded. However, these neighbors had somewhat different views. We called three neighbors to the stand, and all three testified that Harry's teasing was not meanness at all but simply Harry's unusual way of showing his fondness for his wife; he wanted to keep her in the limelight, they said. They testified, also, that Jennifer teased right back.

We then put our own expert on the stand, Dr. James Fellows, a man with multiple degrees. He was an expert's expert, and it cost us the big bucks to get him in that witness chair. Spike handled the questioning after the prosecution accepted him as an expert.

"First of all, Doctor, it is accurate, is it not, that we obtained a court order that allowed you to examine the body shortly after Jennifer Jackson's death?"

"Yes, I did examine the body."

"Doctor, can you explain to the jury exactly what physical problem was being endured by Jennifer Jackson?"

"It was a rare nerve disorder. Nerve disorders affect one or more of the body's nervous systems and can potentially impact speech, motor skills, cognitive ability, heart function, and even breathing. In addition to the central nervous system, specific nerve disorders, such as the one suffered by Jennifer Jackson, can involve the autonomic nervous system or the peripheral nervous system."

"Can you explain to the jury what causes this rare condition?"

"A nerve disorder of this kind may be attributed to bodily injury or trauma, long-term substance abuse, or chronic exposure to environmental toxins."

"And from all of those possibilities, can you hone in on Jennifer's particular type and cause?"

"Yes. From my examination of the nerve cells, I determined that Jennifer suffered from traumatic neuromas. A traumatic neuroma is an area of increased sensitivity, and sometimes pain, that develops in the wake of physical trauma to a nerve such as a cut, a needle puncture, or other similar event. After an injury, nerves will attempt to grow back, extending to cover or fill a gap created by the injury. Sometimes, the nerve cells start to grow in a disorderly fashion. They regenerate rapidly and randomly, creating a cluster of nerve cells that fire in all directions instead of a series of aligned fibers that can smoothly send signals about sensations."

"Doctor, is it likely that Jennifer was in constant pain from the neuroma?"

"Not necessarily, but any pressure on the area around the nerve could cause sharp, searing pain and discomfort."

"Doctor, you have described how Jennifer would have likely suffered some pain and discomfort from her neuroma. Is it possible that she could have been unaware of her illness either because she had little identifiable pain or because she bore some pain without actively investigating the cause?"

"Yes. This is not uncommon. It is very possible that Jennifer had pain that had not fully developed that she chose to ignore, or she had a great desire not to complain of pain to her partner because of her desire not to let the problem get in the way of their relationship."

With this, Spike opened up the possibility that Jennifer either was not aware of the risk of harm by Harry's aggressive "tickling" or she had not told Harry of her problem. The State's Attorney could do nothing to dispel these possibilities in his cross-examination. In fact, it was clear to me that he understood very little about our expert's testimony. We successfully intimidated him from a more comprehensive questioning of the doctor.

In his closing, the State's Attorney claimed that a motive had been established – the life insurance money – and a means had been established to commit a murder – knowledge of a condition that Jennifer could not possibly have hidden from her husband. He said that he was certain that the jury would see that Harry knew that Jennifer could not take rough handling because somehow he was aware of the risks, he handled her in a way that he knew would result in her death, and he planned to profit by her death by increasing the amount of life insurance on her shortly before her death.

Spike's closing argument was quite effective. He pointed out that the prosecution did not have evidence that called for a guilty verdict "beyond a reasonable doubt," as required by the law, since the prosecution had no direct evidence of intent. "In fact," Spike said, "all that the prosecution has proved is that there was an accidental death caused by a man who loved his wife but had an unusual manner of demonstrating his love."

"Teasing is a very undefined word," Spike continued. "Today, we often hear how teasing is meanness among school children. At the same time, don't you remember using teasing among friends as a means of demonstrating your fondness of friends, something to involve your friends in spirited, welcomed communications, an opportunity to bring your friends into the conversation by utilizing humor. Teasing is a childish thing to do. We admit that Harry Jackson was just that, childish, a big kid.

"Let's talk about the insurance issue a moment. Do you seriously think that any insurance agent would admit to a casual upgrading to a million-dollar policy initiated by a client? Do you seriously think that an insurance company would pay off on a policy if it can be proven that a payoff is not necessary because the

140

beneficiary committed a crime that allows the company to keep its money? Not a chance, not if the insurance company can keep its million dollars by having its agent give testimony that makes it appear as though he was virtually forced to write the policy.

"Every bit of so-called evidence presented by the prosecution is mere speculation. There is no proof that Harry Jackson intentionally caused the death of his wife. The judge will tell you that you cannot reach a guilty verdict unless the defendant is found guilty beyond a reasonable doubt. There is no way that you can find this defendant guilty beyond a reasonable doubt."

A surprise ending to the trial came when the jury returned in just twenty minutes. However, we were not really surprised with the verdict: Not Guilty. Harry went free.

FRANK AT 32

In the spring of my first year of teaching I became one of the most popular teachers ever at the school. No, it had nothing to do with my teaching ability. It seems that the baseball coach quit in a huff over a discussion of athletic equipment. The administration said that the school couldn't afford new baseball uniforms while the coach insisted that it was time for the school to incur that cost. The season was set to start in just two weeks when I was asked to stop by the principal's office.

"I'm hearing some good things about your teaching methods," Principal Aaron Jason said.

"Thank you," I replied.

"I wanted to talk to you about a bit of a crises that we have, but first let me ask you this: Did you play some baseball when you were a kid?"

"Sure, all the time, except when I was playing basketball."

"I don't suppose that you managed a Little League team somewhere along the way."

"Actually, I did, for a few years, when I was not much more than a kid myself."

"Perfect. Here's the problem: We're two weeks away from the start of the season, and our baseball coach has bailed out. I need you to take over."

"You're kidding," I said, plainly taken aback.

"Nope. Here's a roster, a practice schedule, and a season schedule. You've been tagged."

"I played baseball and I handled ten-year-olds, but I don't know anything about coaching a high school baseball team."

"It's learn as you go," the principal said. "Look, you're young, your athletic, you've learned how to lead in the military, you're new to the school, giving me the right to pick on you, and it pays a few bucks. Are you in – for the good of the school?"

How could I have turned down such a warm, lucrative offer? Now, along with my History class, there I was the baseball coach.

Baseball is a fun game, so it didn't take long for me to get into it. The team, particularly the infield, had real promise. Ray, at third base, had an exceptional glove and a dependable stick. He had a good eye and made contact. The shortstop, Randy, was incredible in his position. He moved laterally very well and scooped up anything hit near him with great confidence. He was thin and looked a bit brittle, but his bright red head of hair flashed with him as he gathered up ground balls and threw accurately to first base. My catcher, Al, was also a good one with the glove. Best of all, Al could hit the ball a mile; he was knocking down the fence when he wasn't hitting the balls over the fence.

Formidable, I thought, even if the rest of the team was basically mediocre. The season went very well, primarily because of Ray, Randy, and Al, and we finished the season with a record that put us in the state tournament.

I made one small observation toward the end of the season that would have ramifications. Al had a girlfriend, one of my History students, who watched every game and then walked off home with catcher Al. They were a good-looking couple, Sandy with her sparkling red hair, the sister of shortstop Randy, and tall, powerful Al, home run hitter extraordinaire.

143

By some miracle, the first-year coach found his team in the semifinals. Timely hitting and splendid fielding by Ray, brilliantly played middle of the field by Randy, and the long balls of Al got us there. That's when the waste matter hit the fan. Al was a no-show for the game, and he was sorely missed. We did eke out a win when Randy laid down a perfect bunt to bring in the winning run, but we left men on base throughout the game that might have scored with some Al at-bats. Cell phones didn't exist at the time, so I scrambled back to the office at school to call our missing catcher. No answer.

I continued to try to contact Al throughout the next day, with the finals set for the day after that. No luck. I quizzed the other kids about Al's absence and talked to office personnel. No sign of Al, and the finals were upon us.

Still no Al as we began to warm up before the game with some batting practice, but then I had the answer. There walking toward the field was Ray hand and hand with Randy's red-headed sister. A broken heart cost us the state title.

Laura did her best to resist convulsive laughter.

"There's no girl-friend stealing in baseball," I told her.

Thank goodness there was no third baseman around to steal my girl friend because that's exactly what Laura had become in a year that featured learning how to teach, learning how to coach baseball, and somehow finding the time to learn how to love. Even with all of the flaws that I brought into the relationship, oddly it flourished. We did the conventional things – movies, theatre (the local, amateur kind mostly), dinners in restaurants. This was no wild ride, no kinky adventure. We became steadfast friends while going very slowly on the romantic side. It was several months before I heard the story of the dismissed fiancé.

They had scheduled and began planning the wedding. She thought that she had found the perfect lifetime partner, but that was before she discovered a massive flaw in his character. Somehow, he had managed to hide his penchant for alcohol and strip clubs. He managed to conceal these activities from her because he traveled extensively for his job. Overnights were always included in the travel plans. Somehow, when he was home, he was the perfect gentleman, but when he was away, he was a constant late-night customer at the big city strip clubs. This was when his love of alcohol showed its face. He spent long hours in the clubs displaying an entirely different personality than the one Laura saw back home.

As they moved toward their wedding date, the stops at the clubs became more frequent and lengthier – and the drinking grew to excessive. Finally, the out-of-town personality overflowed to his home town. One night, while Laura was conducting a parents' night at the high school, her fiancé, less than a month before the scheduled wedding, went to the one club in her home town. He drank heavily that evening and was seen staggering out of the club by Laura's neighbor, lovable but gossipy Mrs. Jones. What on earth she was doing driving in that area is a massive mystery, but there she was.

Consequently, Mrs. Jones was tending her garden the following morning as Laura approached her vehicle in the driveway, heading toward school. The good neighbor promptly admonished Laura for allowing her fiancé to frequent such establishments.

Shocked and confused, Laura confronted her fiancé with the discovery. Who knows but he may have successfully downplayed the event with a lie or two? Maybe some friends had coerced him into an early bachelor's party? Maybe he was simply relaxing after an especially difficult trip and was not totally aware of the happenings at such a place? Maybe he stopped to see the owner – an old friend – about some business ventures? Alas, no. Instead, he vigorously defended his right to do whatever he pleased; marriage was not to prevent that. Primarily, his defense for drinking and any other immoral behavior was based on his undeniable rights to be free. Laura gave him his freedom.

Having been burned once, Laura became cautious in her relationships. Clearly, my past life would not encourage a nomination for sainthood, but the past few years of turning my life around appeared to reflect well on Laura's opinion of me. In truth, I had been a solid individual - sober, hardworking, conscientious, and considerate. Maybe that nomination would come after all. In any case, Laura liked me and trusted me. I gave her every reason for that trust by continuing as an extraordinary friend with few moments that went beyond that.

Imagine my surprise, consequently, when we had this conversation:

Laura: We need to talk.

Me: Oh, oh, I don't like the sound of that.

Laura: Thanks for being my friend, but maybe we're seeing each other too much?

Me: As the teenagers would say: Are you breaking up with me?

Laura: It's not you. It's me.

Me: I may have heard that line somewhere.

Her whole point was that her heart was broken once, and she didn't want it to happen again. How did I respond to this turn of events? I proposed, declaring my love for her forever and promising that I would never do anything that would bring her embarrassment or regret. My promise was sincere and she knew it. She said yes.

TONY AT 33

My first year as a prosecuting attorney was truly remarkable. Now I was a salaried employee, no longer hustling for clients, criminal or civil. Oddly enough, I wasn't resented for jumping in ahead of four experienced prosecutors. The real prize was the new State's Attorney. Everyone knew that we were a team. We arrived in the office by Spike overwhelming his opponent, the former State's Attorney, in the election. Sure, Spike still had that oratorical gift that he possessed from childhood. His personal appearances in front of community groups, his service as a prosecutor before he left the office, his success in private practice, and his insistence on running a positive campaign all resulted in an easy win.

I thought that Spike was an exceptional State's Attorney, handling both criminal and civil matters pressed upon him in his sphere of responsibility with efficiency and aplomb. That is, until a familiar face was charged with a crime: Brad Wilson, he of the smirking continence who winked at his wife while testifying on her behalf. As you will remember, Charlotte Wilson was the defendant in a DUI death case. Of course, neither Spike nor I were proud of the fact that he was an effective defense witness because he testified quite successfully that he threatened to kill his wife, a reason for her fleeing drunk in a car at a high rate of speed resulting in a death.

This time, Brad Wilson was the defendant. He was accused of being the driver of a vehicle that ran off the road and turned over, killing his passenger, a young woman. True to his character, he was drunk and had walked away from the crash. The woman was behind the wheel when police arrived at the scene. Brad was gone. His story was that he was never there. The police, who spotted him staggering along a country road less than a mile from the crash scene, didn't agree. He was charged with the very same charge that was visited upon his wife not that much earlier: aggravated DUI resulting in a death, right along with a charge of leaving the scene of a fatality, both serious charges. After admitting, after all, that he had been in the car, he insisted that she was the drunk driver. Indeed, there was no question that she had a high alcohol blood content, as did he.

At first, Spike and I pondered whether we should recuse ourselves from prosecuting the case because of our history of defending his wife. We decided that no appeals court would find that we were prejudiced in favor of the defendant since he was only a witness, not a party, in the original case. In addition, he and Charlotte, the former defendant, were alienated, even with a two-month-old baby now in the family. Frankly, we couldn't wait to prosecute this guy.

It wasn't a slam dunk. We had to prove that he was the driver but had placed the woman's body behind the wheel before abandoning the scene. He stuck with the story that the woman, not he, was the drunk driver.

Of course, it was unconstitutional for us to put him on the stand to testify against himself, but we did the second-best thing: We put an expert phrenologist on the stand, a state policeman.

"Your name, please," Spike said.

"Captain Adam Link," he answered. I loved his name, because he was our link to proving Wilson guilty. Spike followed with questions to demonstrate Link's background as an expert, and the defense had to agree that, indeed, he was an expert in interpreting DNA evidence.

"Did your team examine the vehicle that contained the body of Lois Carson?" Spike asked.

"Yes, we did," the Captain responded.

"Please tell us where you found blood in the vehicle."

"There was quite a bit of blood on the seat and against the dashboard on both the driver and passenger sides of the vehicle," Captain Link said.

Sitting next to Spike at the prosecution table, I casually looked toward the courtroom's spectators. There she was, Charlotte, Wilson's alienated wife. She was not smiling and definitely not winking. I wondered now how she felt about the man who beat her, rescued her with his testimony, and then abandoned her and her child.

"And did you find Lois Carson's blood on either side?" Spike continued with his questioning.

"Blood belonging to Lois Carson was found on both seats, driver's and passenger's, as well as on the dashboard and the windshield on the passenger side."

"Did you find any evidence of the defendant's blood on either side of the vehicle?"

"We certainly did. There was just a small amount of blood on the dashboard on the driver's side."

The arresting police officer was next to testify: Sgt. Monroe Dixon. I handled the questioning, which, in part, contained this question: "Sgt. Dixon, at the time you arrested the defendant, did you notice whether he was injured in any way?"

"Yes," Dixon said. "He had an enormous lump on his forehead, and it was clear that he had cut his face just below the left eye."

Thank goodness for DNA capability. We didn't have to demonstrate further that Wilson was driving the car. Of course,

Spike reiterated that fact in his closing argument, but I think that the jury was already convinced of Wilson's guilt before we arrived at that point in the trial.

That was a day that I was especially pleased to be a prosecutor instead of a defense lawyer. If ever there was someone deserving of a guilty verdict and, later, a sentence of six years in prison, that person was Brad Wilson.

* * *

I handled one case during that year that did not involve Spike, but it did involve my old friend, newly married Frank. As a decorated war veteran and successful teacher, Frank was asked to come back to our high school to give the commencement address. Spike and I agreed that he was a wonderful choice. So often, the commencement speaker is a local businessman, politician, or academic. The school wanted someone who could talk about personal experiences in world affairs, about overcoming great obstacles in his personal life, and someone who was involved in education. That was Frank.

Spike, Ellen, Barbara, and I, along with Frank's new wife, Laura, were invited to hear the address along with about 200 high school kids and many parents. As we sat in an auditorium in great anticipation, we heard a commotion coming from off-stage and, then, to everyone's horror, a gunshot. We learned later that a teenager who failed to graduate because he was expelled from the school earlier in his senior year had entered the side door of the auditorium just as everyone was getting seated. He shared the offstage area with everyone who was to participate in the commencement – the students who were Valedictorian and Salutatorian, the principal, a member of the faculty who was serving as emcee, and Frank. Suddenly the teenager pulled a pistol from his jacket pocket.

Everyone, save one, froze, but Frank leaped at him and drove him to the floor. The gun fired a bullet into the ceiling as Frank wrestled him to the floor and finally took the gun away from him. Of course, the boy was arrested and dragged off by the police. How Frank had the nerves to deliver the commencement address after that incident was simply illustrative of the courage and quick thinking that helped him survive his war experiences. The emcee briefly explained that there was an incident offstage that was handled by the police and that there was no need to be concerned. The graduation ceremony continued.

Spike and I were thrilled with Frank's commencement speech about tenacity and setting goals in life, about the necessity of continuing one's education for a lifetime, and about the importance of high morals and kindness throughout one's career. I smiled, thinking of the three of us as not all that dedicated to those ideals when we were trouble-making kids.

I was assigned to pursue charges against the boy. Johnny Sparks had been just a little off kilter most of his life. As is almost always the case with young men who somehow go awry, he was a loner, not active in sports or other extracurricular activities at school. In class, he was a dreamer but somehow managed decent marks along the way. Over six feet tall with massive shoulders, he might have been an athlete if he chose to do so, but he simply had no interest. The problem leading to high school expulsion was his short fuse. He had several run-ins with the principal because of mouthing off to his teachers when they had the audacity to give him concrete instructions on behavior in the classroom. Finally, he had gotten into an altercation not with a teacher or another boy but with a female student. Emma and he had glared at each other across the classroom over some disagreement a few minutes earlier in the lunch room. As the bell rang to end the class, he dashed to Emma and slapped her across the face. Several students pulled him away from her. The ruckus was heard by the principal who happened to be going by in the corridor. He was a former athlete, a college football player. With students hollering to him with a report of the attack on Emma, the principal grabbed Johnny, twisted an arm behind him, and pinned him against the wall until he had calmed down. He was expelled the following day, and his seething vengeance was then aimed at the principal.

His attorney was the public defender, John Mills, the former State's Attorney who had been evicted from office by Spike being elected to the job. Public defenders and other defense lawyers often come from the ranks of lawyers trained as prosecutors who either lose their jobs or decide that defense work is more lucrative. In Mills' case, he wasn't a very successful prosecutor and was now a defense lawyer because of his lost reelection. He became the public defender because no one else wanted the job.

Johnny was charged with attempted murder, although I knew that the charge might not stick, as well as possessing a firearm without a license and firing a gun in a public place.

A few days after the arraignment, Mills called me for a meeting.

"Look, Tony," Mills said, "the kid tells me that all he wanted to do was put a scare into the principal. He says he got the gun out of his father's desk drawer and had no idea that it was loaded."

"He didn't know it was loaded?" I replied. "Come on, John, surely you don't believe that."

"Nevertheless, he didn't intend to shoot it. It went off when your friend tackled him. If that hadn't happened, he would have waved the gun around to frighten everyone. That's all he was trying to do."

"The kid needs major help," I said, "the mental health kind."

"Exactly," Mills said. "Let's get these charges dismissed and get him some time in a, you know, nut house."

152

"I'm sure the people involved would rather have it called a mental health facility," I responded.

"Whatever. That's what he needs, not a criminal record."

"What he did was extremely dangerous. More than one person could have died by his actions. I'm grateful that Frank was there, even if you do blame him for the gun discharging."

"All right, all right, but do you want to send this kid to prison or do you want to get this kid straightened out?"

"Maybe both. I want to talk to Frank about exactly what he saw when he jumped the kid. Do the parents have the money to provide some professional mental health care? You're here representing him as the public defender, so they didn't come up with any money to help defend him."

"The old man's got money," Mills said. "The kid has reached maturity and he doesn't live home; he was living in a two by four apartment and working in a grocery store. The parents are divorced, but I think the husband has been helping the kid out, probably gave him some money."

"Obviously he had access to his father's office," I said.

"Yeah, he'd run errands for his father sometimes."

"I'll get back to you after I talk to Frank, but I'll tell you, this is no little matter because teenagers shouldn't have guns."

I asked Frank to stop by when he could. The following Saturday morning, we met in my office.

"Frank," I said, "these are serious charges. I can't let a drawn gun in a school go unpunished. He's going to jail at least. The biggest issue I have is whether he intended to kill the principal."

"I've thought about that," Frank answered. "I couldn't read his mind, but I'm guessing that he was looking for a lot of attention without any thought of consequences. When he pulled the gun from his jacket, he pointed it up toward the ceiling and waved it around, getting everyone's attention, including mine. I was about ten feet away from him."

"Okay, at that point, he wanted everyone to see him. He says he wanted to frighten the principal, that's all. What we don't know is whether he would have then brought the gun down and shot the principal. Was waving the gun around to create fear his only goal or did he intend to follow through with a shooting after he got everyone's attention?"

"Can't help you there, buddy. I didn't want to find out. I'll tell you, though, he sure looked surprised when the gun went off."

"He says he didn't know the gun was loaded," I said. "I doubted that, but maybe he didn't."

"It's possible," Frank said. "That's one of the many dangers of guns. People get shot all the time by 'unloaded' guns."

A few days later, I had Mills back in the office.

"Here's the deal, John," I said. "Johnny pleads guilty to unlawful possession and discharge of a weapon in a public place and you get his father to consent to getting Johnny some urgent mental health care during his jail term. After he agrees to that and Johnny pleads guilty to the lesser charges, I'll drop the attempted murder charge and recommend a year in jail to the judge."

Mills was ecstatic. "You'd do that for the kid?"

"Get his father on board with the idea. I'll pull strings with the sheriff to arrange the mental health sessions while he's still in jail. There's too much of this business of putting people away without an explanation about what the mental disturbance is all about. Let's see if we can do something about this one."

Spike approved the deal. As I expected, though, he cautioned me that we were taking an enormous risk that the kid couldn't get straightened out. There's no question that I was jittery about it. I had nightmares about him getting out of jail and shooting up a school or a shopping mall sometime down the road. Spike also correctly pointed out that it was likely that our office would be roundly criticized by the public for not sending Johnny to prison for a long time.

I gulped at that one, too, but decided to stay with what I thought was right. We got the guilty plea and the commitment from Johnny's father to finance psychological help for his son. The judge sent him to the county jail for a year, less a day, and I moved on, but the case cost me some sleepless nights praying that Johnny could be turned around by the mental health care professionals before he left jail.

That's when I decided that my tenure as a prosecutor would be a short one. Maybe I wasn't tough enough to be a prosecutor; I thanked Spike and, despite his protestations, I went back to the defense side.

TONY AT 34

Yes, Barbara and I wanted children. We discussed and dreamed about the possibility for about five years and then actively pursued that goal for another three years or so. During the first few years of our marriage, we were both busy. Then, for a period, Barbara was home and bored, trying to get pregnant. Then, she went back to teaching while I went from defense/plaintiff's lawyer to prosecutor back to defense lawyer.

We went so far as to have a doctor determine whether there might be a problem in Barbara getting pregnant, either on my side or hers. We even talked about in vitro fertilization if it were determined that we couldn't do it on our own. As it turned out, we didn't need any help.

"Want to go shopping for furniture?" she asked one evening.

"What do we need?" I asked.

"Baby furniture."

"You mean …"-

"Yes. I was at the doctor's this afternoon. The kid is on his/her way."

"Yikes! Are we ready for this?" I said, totally flabbergasted.

"Are you kidding me? Teenagers are ready for this kind of thing. We're way overdue, buddy."

To my amazement, I had two phone calls that month, one from Spike and one from Frank. In essence, the news was the same – three old friends, each with a wife who was expecting a first child. Unbelievable!

Both Ellen and Laura were having pregnancies that were seemingly uneventful. For Barbara, it wasn't so easy. Only seven months pregnant, she had to be admitted to the hospital with what was then called toxemia, now referred to as pre-eclampsia. There were discussions of forcing an early birth. Amazingly, I thought, the discussions were between the doctors and didn't seem to involve us until I let them know that we wanted to be informed of what was happening. Only then did Barbara's pediatrician explain the problem as being life-threatening with eclampsia, if it went that far, possibly causing seizures. His recommendation was to induce labor. Of course, we were also concerned as to how this would affect the baby, but I was more concerned about Barbara getting through this all right, even if it meant losing the baby.

Inducing labor didn't work even though it was attempted over a period that kept her in the hospital for thirty days, so she was discharged with the pre-eclampsia ameliorated to a degree anyway. After a fretful week at home, she was returned to the hospital where the doctor performed a Caesarian birth. The baby, a girl, was perfect in every way – and so was Barbara. Not so small a problem, however: Barbara was home for just a week, during which we began to learn how to care for a baby when she had terrific stomach pains. I called 911 and an ambulance arrived. Off she went back to the hospital where they removed her appendix.

While my heart went out to her for all she had been through, there I was primarily responsible for the care of a newly born baby while she was at the hospital and while she was recuperating.

Bless my mother who was 78 at the time but had raised eleven children. She spent part of the next four days with me demonstrating the technical aspects of caring for a baby – bottle preparation and feeding, diaper changing, how to hold, and, yes, burp a baby, and what to do with that messy diaper. This was before extensive use of disposable diapers, so it was an edifying experience. When Barbara arrived back home from the hospital, I helped a bit, with all of my new-found knowledge, but she took charge and put her problems behind her.

So, what did we get out of all this effort? A beautiful girl that we named Mary Lynn. The fact that her initials, MLB, also stood for Major League Baseball, was primarily a coincidence.

"You know what, Tony," Barbara said, "she was worth the thirty days in the hospital, the trip back for the Caesarian, even the appendectomy."

"She's even worth the diaper changing," I said.

That's when the phone call came from Spike.

"Is all well there?" he asked.

"Couldn't be better," I said. "Have you heard from Frank?"

"Yep. He didn't want to bother you because I've kept him up to date on what's happening and about Barbara's adventures, but you may want to give him a call. Laura just delivered a boy, David Eisenhower Foley. How about that?"

"That's wonderful."

"Oh, and by the way," Spike said, "Ellen wanted to join the party. We had a boy this morning, Daniel Webster Dumbrowski. Ellen's doing great and so is Danny."

TONY AT 36

It is not my intention to use this platform to bring praise to myself for my work as a defense lawyer since leaving the position of First Assistant State's Attorney in Spike's office, but the temptation to relate at least one case of interest is overwhelming, so I will do so.

First, I must admit that Spike and his assistants were exceptional prosecutors. It was my good fortune never to face Spike in an important case. There were occasions, of course, when my office faced off against Spike's, but the matters were usually resolved amicably. The primary reason why we were not at separate tables in the same courtroom was that my practice was primarily in civil cases. An occasional criminal case usually resulted in my facing one of Spike's assistants or in the case never reaching trial because of a well-advised guilty plea.

One of those times when I did take on the State's Attorney's office involved a murder case of some prominence. Again, fortunately for me, Spike's First Assistant State's Attorney, Brian Stallard, was the prosecutor. The defendant, Frederick Stratton, was a well-known businessman, owner of many apartment complexes. Paradoxically, he was a doctor who invested in real estate only to discover that he enjoyed the business of owning apartments over practicing medicine, so he retired as a doctor and became a multi-millionaire in the real estate business. Unbelievably, he was accused of murdering his wife, a woman he had married forty years before the terrible event. In an apparent fit of anger, he had taken a common steak knife and cut her throat (or so he was charged with doing so).

Of course, he was held without bail. I was hired by his oldest son to defend him, so I visited him in his cell.

"Doctor, please tell me what you remember about the death of your wife," I began.

"That's it. I don't remember anything about what happened. They say that I killed her with a knife. Why would I do such a terrible thing? I loved my wife."

"What is the last thing you do remember, Doctor?"

"Please just call me Fred. I gave up medicine a long time ago. What was the last thing I remember? I'm not sure. We were arguing about something. We had arguments, but they were always forgotten immediately."

"About what time was it when you had this argument?"

"It was right after lunch, I think. We had gone to a Taco Bell. The noise was maddening in there. They had some terrible music playing, and it was crowded with customers talking loudly to speak above the sound of the music."

"Yes, Fred, go ahead."

"She was telling me some annoying story about somebody I don't know and don't care about, something about how this person's daughter had died but her ashes hadn't been buried and six months had gone by. I had heard it all before, so I told her that I could do without hearing it all over again."

"Did this anger her?"

"Yes. She told me that I never listened to her, that I didn't really care about her, and all I cared about was my apartments."

"Was that true?" I asked.

"Of course not. It's just that she's so annoying when she insults me like that. Sometimes, I seethe about it for the rest of the day."

160

"And after you arrived home from lunch, what do you remember then?"

"Nothing. All I can remember is a policeman nudging me. I was sitting in the corner of the room. I saw that I was splattered with blood. Then I saw her lying on the floor in the middle of the room. They had covered her face with a sheet, but of course I knew it was her. I don't know what happened. How could they think I did that awful thing?"

"Is there anything, anything at all that you can remember from after lunch until the police officer roused you – an image of some kind, a dream-like vision, a picture that crosses your mind? Anything?"

"I think … I think I remember doing something with my hands. There was a loaf of bread in my hands. I was… cutting the bread."

The McNaughton Rule is the existing defense of insanity. Basically, it says that an individual is not guilty of a crime if he or she did not understand the nature of the act. Paradoxically, the example typically given by law professors in a criminal law class in law school is a person slitting a throat thinking that he or she is slicing a loaf of bread. McNaughton was not only the appropriate defense, it actually fit the example that defined the rule!

The real question in my mind was whether my client, Dr. Stratton, knew about the McNaughton Rule. Also troubling was why he could remember everything a while before and after his wife's death but had no memory for that short window of time just before, during, and immediately after his wife's death. At the same time, I was not about to assume that Fred was the knife wielder. The prosecution had to prove that.

161

And they did. The homicide detective was the first to testify at the trial.

"Detective, please describe what you saw when you arrived at the scene of the crime," Stallard said.

"Mrs. Stratton's body was on the floor in the middle of the living room. Her throat had been cut. There was a steak knife a few feet from the body."

"Was there blood on the knife and did the police lab determine that it was Mrs. Stratton's blood?"

"Yes to both questions," the detective said.

"And were there fingerprints on the knife?" Stallard asked.

"Yes. There was only one set of fingerprints. They belonged to the defendant, Dr. Stratton."

The prosecution established that Dr. Stratton was the only person in the home – no servants, no relatives, no workers. A neighbor who sat on her front porch facing the main entrance of the Stratton home testified that she saw the Strattons returning home from lunch and saw no one else go in or leave the home that afternoon. For what it was worth, the prosecution also established that Dr. Stratton was his wife's sole beneficiary of a life insurance policy and of her estate.

Of course, we had a psychiatrist testify for the defense. He had examined Dr. Stratton and interviewed him about what he remembered about that tragic afternoon.

"Dr. Clark," I said, after we had established his expertise, "please tell the jury what Dr. Stratton told you about his recollection of the afternoon of April 20th."

That was a big question, considering the fact that Dr. Clark spoke with Dr. Stratton over a period of two hours. However, I knew exactly what Dr. Stratton had told Dr. Clark about that afternoon. The remainder of the time spent with the defendant was really a mental examination.

"He told me that he had no direct memory of anything from shortly after he arrived back home with his wife from lunch until the time he was roused into consciousness by a police officer."

"Dr. Clark, is this possible?"

"Yes, it is."

"So we're talking about amnesia here, is that right?" I asked.

"Possibly a form of amnesia. Amnesia refers to the loss of memories, such as information and experiences. It's not as portrayed in the movies; real-life amnesia generally doesn't cause a loss of self-identity. I have diagnosed Dr. Stratton with a form of amnesia called transient global amnesia."

"Please define transient global amnesia," I said.

"It is a sudden, temporary episode of memory loss. During an episode of transient global amnesia, the recall of recent events simply vanishes. The sufferer may draw a blank when asked to remember something that happened a day, a month, or even a year ago, or, in Dr. Stratton's case, something that happened only minutes before."

"Is this, then, a permanent loss of memory for a particular time span?"

"Paradoxically, the loss of memory for the specific time period is permanent, but further episodes are rare and unlikely to happen again."

"Doctor," I then asked, "what is the cause of transient global amnesia?"

"Any form of amnesia can result from damage to brain structures that form the limbic system, which controls your emotions and memories. These structures include the thalamus, which lies deep within the center of your brain, and the hippocampal formations, which are situated within the temporal lobes of your brain."

"Okay, Doctor, but in simpler terms for me and the jury, what exactly causes this disorder?"

"There could be any number of causes but most likely would be a stroke, a lack of adequate oxygen in the brain, for example, from a heart attack or respiratory distress, or from long-term alcohol abuse leading to a vitamin B-1 deficiency."

"Of these, based on your examination of Dr. Stratton, which was the most likely cause for his condition?"

"We extended our examination to include physical abnormalities. He did not have a heart attack. There was no indication of respiratory disease. We did discover, however, that Dr. Stratton was a heavy drinker, especially after he left the practice of medicine. It is my professional opinion that the transient global amnesia was caused by alcoholism."

I do believe that First Assistant State's Attorney Stallard's head was spinning. He had failed to uncover Dr. Stratton's alcohol problem and, worse, had no idea that transient global amnesia existed. He passed on cross-examination.

Establishing that Dr. Stratton didn't remember killing his wife wasn't good enough, however. Normally, being intoxicated would not excuse someone from committing a crime under the theory of not knowing what he or she was doing. For example, driving while drunk or, worse, killing someone in a drunk driving crash is not excusable; the offender chose to put himself or herself in that condition, so the individual is culpable for whatever occurs afterward as a result. We had to put Dr. Stratton on the stand.

"Doctor, I understand that you prefer to be called Mr. rather than Doctor. Is that correct?"

"Yes, I gave up my license some time ago. Mister is fine."

"We need to talk about that terrible afternoon when your wife died. Is it your contention that you have no memory of that afternoon?"

"Yes, it is," Stratton replied. "I can't remember anything from the time we returned from lunch to the time I was roused by the police officer. I can't believe what I was seeing, my wife dead there on the floor."

"Now, Mister Stratton, even though you have no specific memory of that time period, isn't it true that, in fact, you do remember yourself going through some activity even though it was more of a dream than an action?"

"Yes, that's something that I don't understand, but I do have this kind of hazy image in my mind of something very unusual."

"What did you see in this hazy image?"

"I was slicing a loaf of bread but not on a table or cutting board. I was holding it in the crook of one arm and slicing it toward me."

Stallard could accomplish no more on cross-examination. Stratton only repeated what he said on direct examination.

My closing argument had to piece all of this together, a story that invited skepticism and disbelief. Nevertheless, the best I could do was emphasize what the testimony indicated: He was insane as defined by the insanity defense, and, as the result of his insane act, combined with his alcoholism, he had developed a transient global amnesia that erased the insane act from his mind.

Stallard stressed the unbelievability of the story and the unlikely affliction, he said, of the temporary memory loss. He questioned the coincidence of the victim's throat being slashed in a way that was precisely the example typically used to describe an act of someone who was insane. Frankly, I had no idea which way the jury would go, and jury deliberations extended well into the evening.

The wait for a jury decision was torturous. Jury members had heard from an expert witness of an odd but temporary form of amnesia, and the jury had to believe that Stratton was insane at the time of the killing under the concept of a rule that was new to them, the McNaughton Rule. They had to believe Mr.

Stratton when he testified that he had no memory of the death of his wife and that he thought that he was slicing a loaf of bread, not cutting a throat, because he was temporarily insane. At the same time, I thought that some jurors would not believe Mr. Stratton at all, that he was lying about both his memory and the violent act of killing his wife.

He was found not guilty by reason of insanity. He was held at a hospital for the criminally insane until psychiatrists were convinced that he wasn't a danger to himself or to others, a period of some eight months after the trial. Shortly after his release, he sold all of his property and moved to Wisconsin to be near the son who hired me to defend him. I wondered if it would not have been better if he had developed a permanent form of amnesia to forget about the entire experience.

This was an extremely odd case and one that will always leave me with this question: Did I get it right with my amnesia and insanity defense or did the retired doctor get away with murder?

FRANK AT 44

I loved teaching. Although I spent most of my early life convinced that I was meant to be a career soldier, I was now certain that teaching was my true calling. I also loved Laura. In the first three years of our marriage, we had two children, both boys. David was a husky, scrappy, bright nine-year-old. Mark, almost a carbon copy of his brother, was seven. Unlike my father who fancied himself a disciplinarian when I was a boy, I was a cupcake. I gave the boys almost anything they wanted, sometimes against Laura's advice. However, I never quite got over my Army experience, so when there was any aspect of being tough with the boys, it harkened back to my Army training. Laura, David, and Mark tactfully ridiculed my use of Army terms. They remained a part of my vocabulary. A jail was still the stockade, we lived in a billet, we went on maneuvers when we went camping, and we sometimes ate at the mess hall.

There was one instance when David had messed up at school. He had spoken up when good sense would have kept him quiet. He explained it this way: "It was the principal's fault," he said. "Our history teacher used one class to tell us about some history of music. It was a great class. He was telling us about the beginning of rock 'n' roll. He played a record by a group called Bill Haley and the Comets. The principal came in and said we were being too noisy."

"Did your teacher turn down the volume?"

"No, he turned it up. That's when the principal gave the teacher the rest of the day off. He said that if we wanted to know about the history of music, we should be listening to guys named Beethoven and Mozart. I told him that we weren't interested in that old junk. Some of the other kids started yelling yeah, yeah. That's when he told me that if I wanted to make decisions for the class, I needed to be a good leader. He said that a good leader is an informed leader, so he gave me a bunch of reading to do and some music to listen to."

"Okay. I guess you had better get started on it. Looks like he's set up an early warning system for the class. You're it."

"I have to do this?" he asked.

"What are your alternatives?" I responded.

"Maybe some damage control," he said. Damage control. Where did this kid get phrases like that?

He suggested to the principal that the school establish a Hit Parade Club outside of school hours where his teacher could talk about rock 'n' roll as well as any other form of music, including the "old guys" music. The principal liked the idea, the teacher liked the idea, and the kids at his school got to listen to a great variety of music once a week after school but mostly rock 'n' roll.

I was impressed with the way David handled the "damage control" and turned it into a good experience for him and his friends. "Good officer material," I thought to myself.

Mark, in the meantime, was clearly envious of his brother's demonstration of leadership.

"I think I'm going to cause a little rumble in my class," he said. I warned him.

Laura and I continued to teach at Plattsburg High School, but my one year of coaching baseball was enough; the school hired a real coach. Instead, both of us were involved in voluntary assistance in after-school programs, enjoying the company of our neighbors and friends, and – sky diving.

I never thought that I could convince Laura to try it, but she agreed. I had jumped a number of times while I was in the Army. I thought that it would be much more fun to jump as a civilian, and there would be the bonus of jumping with other fans of sky diving. With Laura's permission, of course (I didn't want to worry her), I joined the local club and made a few jumps. That's when I asked Laura if she wanted to give it a try. I was shocked when she agreed with very little coaxing.

I let the professionals do Laura's training on Saturday morning. I went along for moral support.

"First, we're going to watch a video," the instructor, Rocky Hilton, said. "Then, we're going to walk out to our Beechcraft and practice the jump. I'll need you to sign some liability release papers, though, before we go too far."

Laura blinked at that last line. I had assured her that there was little risk.

After the video, I stood in the back of the pack as Rocky talked to Laura and four other first-time jumpers.

"We're going to take up three of you on the first trip, two on the second. Laura, Mike, Ed, why don't you three get into the plane."

I was amazed at how cool and collected Laura was. The three climbed up a few steps into the plane.

"Now, I'm going to show you exactly what's going to happen," Rocky said. "Jim is going to be the pilot and I'll be your jump commander. You will have a chute on and will also be packed with an emergency chute. You will also be wired so that Kevin can communicate with you from the ground. When I tap you, you do this."

At this point, Rocky stepped on a ledge and placed one hand and then the other on the holding bar beneath the wing. "That's step one," he said. "Then you will step off the ledge so that you'll be dangling from the crossbar, holding on with your hands."

"You're kidding," said Mike, one of the first-time jumpers.

"Nope. That's how it's done until you're really comfortable with jumping. Now, when you're out there, successfully dangling, you simply let go. The whoosh of the wind will carry you away from the plane and will open your chute. Then all you do is enjoy the ride to the ground. Okay?"

"Ah, why do we have that other chute?" Mike asked.

"When you get your jump suit on, I'm going to show you the location of a rip cord. If once in a billion, your chute doesn't open, that's the baby that opens a second chute. If that happens, we'll be hollering at you from the ground. Not to worry."

"How long does it take to get to the ground?" Ed asked.

"Oh, it's a nice five-to-ten-minute ride," Rocky said. "Enjoy. But now we're going to do a few practice landings. I'll teach you how to hit the ground rolling and how to gather your chute. Today, though, the guys on the ground will give you a hand with that last part."

About a half-hour later, up went the plane with Laura, Mike, and Ed as new sky divers. I stood at the edge of the field with my large video camera, propped up on my shoulder. It occurred to me that even though I had jumped now more than a few times, I had never watched anyone else jump while I was on the ground. The plane seemed to be much higher than I expected.

To my surprise, Laura was the first to come out of the airplane. (I learned later that Ed decided at the last minute not to go out.) She was just a speck in the sky as her chute opened. Then, immediate concern, because she made a few circles in the sky, but she immediately adjusted as per the instructions by pulling the strings on one side of the parachute. I breathed easier as she descended slowly to the ground, making a perfect landing. *She may be better at this than I am*, I thought.

"Terrific," I said as I ran to her. "Great job!"

"If you think I'm ever going to do this again," she said, "you would be right. Let's go back up."

"Hey, you're kidding. This isn't a carnival ride. Maybe next week."

Sure enough, we were there the next week and the week after that. After several more jumps, we felt okay about David and Mark watching. Of course, they were excited.

"Looking good up there," David said.

"Hey, how about me?" I asked.

"We expect you to be insane," he said, "not Mom."

Mark was even more enthusiastic: "Way to go, Mom!"

That's how Laura caught the fever. Much to the shock and amusement of our friends, Laura and I became monthly sky divers, improving in technique, jumping from higher heights, learning to pack our own chutes. Then, one fateful Saturday morning, we called it quits. That morning, one of our friends somehow got tangled in the chute. It shouldn't have happened. It couldn't have happened. But it did. We were looking on, ready to take the next plane up when it happened. It was the first loss of a life since the beginning of the club. At the funeral, we simply looked at each other and knew that we didn't want David and Mark to grow up without a parent. We were done with sky diving.

After that, we assumed a much more normal life, concentrating more on our sons than on ourselves. That's when we became actively concerned with a playground situation that came to our attention.

The boys had friends not only at their school but also in a neighboring town because of their active participation in YMCA sports. What we heard from them was that a number of younger brothers and sisters had contacted a rare form of cancer. There had been extensive investigation by local authorities seeking the cause, knowing that there had to be a common exposure of the children that brought on the cancer. There was no definite answer except that some parents realized that the children affected had all spent considerable time at the same playground. It was also observed that the playground was adjacent to but at a distance from a fenced chemical plant.

With the parents' approval, I called upon the two best lawyers that I knew, Spike and Tony. There had been a surprising development in Spike's career. He had resigned from his State's Attorney position to run for Governor! Once again, he had been approached by party leaders who thought that he would be the best candidate for the ticket. He did not want to begin full-time campaigning for the primary, yet he wanted to stay busy, so he joined his old friend, Tony, as Of Counsel for his firm. This team was perfect for me and for the families of my sons' friends. Spike and Tony took on the chemical company to prove that chemical leaking from the plant had caused cancer in the kids. All three of us knew that this would be an almost insurmountable task. Nevertheless, Spike hired investigators who determined that, yes, chemicals waste dumped by the company had permeated the ground onto the children's playground.

Because of the possibility of further instances of cancer, Spike was able to obtain an expedited trial date, much to the grief of the chemical company. The most remarkable aspect of this was that Spike, still the magic tongue, talked the company into a settlement even though there was no certainty that there was a causal connection between the cancer and the dumping!

The quick settlement was accomplished because the company feared a jury verdict that would have resulted in millions and millions of dollars to the impacted families. Instead, the company agreed to pay mere millions to the families and to finance the building of a new playground at a safe site while razing the old playground and cleaning up the area and taking steps to avoid further pollution.

Because I initiated the action and brought Spike and Tony into the litigation, I was also considered to be something of a hero, a fact that put me in a good light – deservedly or not – in the eyes of the community and of my impressed wife and sons. I was on a high. As David put it, my "early warning system was in gear," and I had exercised "splendid damage control."

SPIKE AT 44

Even though I was the local party leaders' candidate, I still had to run against two other candidates in the state primary. One was a State Senator, the other a multimillionaire industrialist. Tony and Frank assisted me in my campaign. They did an amazing job of getting my homely face plastered throughout the state on billboards, buying TV time, and raising money to pay for it all. Since I had made friends on both sides of the courtroom, many lawyers also helped promote me to lead the ticket. But at times, I thought, *what was I doing here?*

The State Senator was well liked and a political insider. His name was Benton Godfrey. I had seen him in action when I testified several times on bills initiated by the State's Attorneys' Association. He was to-the-point brisk, highly intelligent, and a leader. At 60, he appeared to be a bit war torn and older than his age. Just a little on the heavy side, one would have guessed that he spent considerable hours in fine dining. His striking characteristic, however, was his totally unkempt, thick eyebrows. Each hair seemed to determine its own direction, and there were many of them with virtually no separation above a formidable nose. When watching him or even speaking with him, it was difficult not to be drawn visually to that area of his face.

Another distinct advantage for Godfrey was a resonant voice that could thunder whenever that effect was worthwhile. He had been a law professor for a few decades before running for office. The word was that he terrorized freshmen students who were foolish enough to come to class unprepared. I knew that he was going to be a difficult opponent and that our one scheduled debate would be a challenge for me.

Myron Linton, the wealthy industrialist, now 55, was Godfrey's almost exact opposite in many ways. He was short and slim. *A pipsqueak*, flashed across my mind involuntarily. His voice was high pitched and basically annoying. His sharp nose and semi-closed eyes portrayed a man who was always deep in thought. One's first assumption was that surely his smallish head was overcrowded with an enormous brain. Unbelievably, he was almost a millionaire before he left high school, having invested funds left to him by his grandparents with his no-clue father as the errand boy and temporary guardian of the growing profits. Since the highlight of my financial career was successfully balancing my checkbook each month, I would attempt to avoid most economics discussions during the debate.

Sometime during the campaigning for the nomination, I ran into Godfrey on the steps of the courthouse. I'm not sure that I'll ever understand the conversation that took place, but it went something like this:

"You're rather young to be in this race, aren't you?" he said for openers.

"Relatively young, I suppose," I said, "but I'm energetic and looking forward to the job." At this, he raised his formidable eyebrows.

"I believe you were in high school when I was a law professor if I'm not mistaken."

"Sorry I missed you at the law school. Perhaps I'll learn a thing or two from you at the debate."

"No doubt," he said, "no doubt. Come prepared."

Great, I thought, *I'll have one guy trying to teach me law and another grilling me about finance and economics. Maybe I should have stood in bed as the saying goes.*

Working the chemical leak case with Tony had actually been a respite prior to what became an ugly campaign. On at least a few occasions, I harkened back to murder cases as Dickens' "best of times" with the campaign quickly becoming the "worst of times."

I suppose it all began with an announcement from the squeaky multimillionaire that I had "deserted" my post as a prosecutor to defend a man accused of murder. Not only that, it was "apparent" that I preferred to represent criminals. Of course, neither accusation made sense. At that point in my life, I had represented the State in multiple prosecutions of criminals, had indeed represented some charged with a crime (but some, like Frank, who were totally innocent of the charges), and had represented plaintiffs in civil actions. Did I "prefer" to defend criminals? Even I didn't know the answer to that question. Nevertheless, that's what the industrialist said, and I'm sure that many voters believed him. Lies, even exaggerations, will be believed by many if they are said often enough. Didn't Adolf Hitler obtain his power in exactly that way?

Then bushy brows got into it with his electronic campaign. His TV ad said that both Myron Linton and I were "aristocratic." He pointed to Linton's tight control over his industrial "empire" and my autocratic running of the State's Attorney's Office. Nonsense. In fact, that was a major issue of elections back in the John Adams and Thomas Jefferson elections. At least Godfrey was observant of history.

I chose the high road. Never did I criticize or even mention one of my opponents in any of my ads. The whole business of negative advertising sickened me. Foolishly or not, I decided not to swing back but simply take the punches with confidence in voters that they would ascertain whether what my opponents were saying about me had any basis of fact. No, my ads pointed out what I had planned for my time in office as Governor. With the help of friends, professionals in various fields, and of course Tony and Frank, we detailed our plans for the economy, for new legislation to combat various State ills, and for cutting taxes if at all possible. We hedged a bit on that last promise, but we made it clear that cutting taxes was going to be a priority effort with the emphasis on effort. Then, the grand debate was on.

Each candidate had the opportunity to speak for three minutes followed by questions from a panel of three reporters to each candidate with each of us having an opportunity to respond to each answer. I won't bore you with a verbatim report, but here, in my estimation, were the highlights.

During those first three minutes, I praised my opponents but briefly and then said: "I will draw upon my legal experience as both a prosecutor and as defense counsel and search out the best advice I can muster to guarantee that I serve the citizens of this state to the best of my ability. Further, I will always tell you the truth, even if it is painful to do so, if I have made any error in representing you while doing my very best." A minute or so later, I said, "I am and will always be aware of the poor, the needy, the disadvantaged, the mentally ill, and I will work with you to bring some relief to those groups. I am and will always be aware of the problems created by criminals, the easy availability of assault weapons, and drunk, reckless, and distracted drivers. I will work with the Legislature in solving those problems."

In response to a question asked by one of the three reporters, Godfrey said, "It seems to me that Mr. Dumbrowski plans to ignore the rights and liberties of our citizens. I believe in adhering to those Constitutional rights, especially those given to us under the Second Amendment."

Give me a break, I thought. *I would like a civilized, safe society while still retaining established rights*, but what I said was, "I am an advocate of Constitutional rights, but these rights include guaranteed safety from criminal and irresponsible behavior."

Linton piped in with a total non sequitur: "Our spending continues to be rampant. How can we offer what Mr. Dumbrowski wants without raising taxes?"

The remainder of the debate was pretty much what you would see and hear in any debate involving candidates for local posts throughout the country. Was I the winner? The newspapers seemed to think so, perhaps in part out of sympathy for me because it appeared that Godfrey and Linton chose to target me for elimination at the polls. It didn't happen. The victory was by a narrow margin, but I went on to represent the party in the election for Governor.

My opponent in that race was the then State Attorney General. He had been touted as the likely candidate for the job four years earlier. To the surprise of almost everyone, he opted not to run at that time against the then Governor who was running for reelection. He also knew that the Governor would not be eligible for another term in four years. Consequently, his strategy was to wait four years to get the nomination. It paid off. He had no competition in the primary.

Attorney General Brent Dodd was tall, lean, and quite serious. When he did attempt to smile for the camera – a rare event – the resulting expression left much to be desired; his smile did not light up the room. Nevertheless, he was a handsome man with an extraordinary amount of thick hair for a 60-year-old. Unfortunately for a politician, however, as intelligent as he proved to be and as articulate as he demonstrated in public appearances, his voice quality was on the edge of shrillness. Perhaps his voice did not affect most others in the same way, but – for me – it was simply annoying. Nevertheless, no one could dispute his work ethic and his accomplishments as the Attorney General. It would be a battle, I figured.

Again, I chose the high road, absolutely no negative campaigning. That, for me, was not only the wise course but was the only logical one; Dodd had no fault that was known to me or any of my campaign staff.

"How about that grin of his," Frank commented. "I really hate to say anything this crass, but the man seems to be passing gas every time he attempts a smile. Why don't we include that picture in some of our advertising?"

"Shame on you, Frank," Tony said, "but that's not a bad idea."

No, I had too much respect for the man to do that to him.

I would summarize the campaign on both sides as basically boring. I don't believe that either of us created an issue that stimulated voters. Dodd did pick up on the Godfrey and Linton comments that I expected to do too much without the clear necessity of raising taxes, but apparently the voters had no problem with casting votes for a candidate with an ambitious program. Oh, there was one other small consideration. Just one week before the election, newspaper photographers captured a few photos of Dodd at about 2:00 a.m. holding his car door open to enable entrance by an oft-arrested working girl. Ouch! I was elected Governor.

TONY AT 52

Spike, Frank, and I had such busy lives that we didn't see each other very much but stayed in contact. Then Spike had the great idea of a vacation reunion – our families included. We picked a location that was more or less half way for all of us, south of Plattsburg where Frank still lived and north of Spike and me in the Albany area.

Of course, we hit the million-dollar beach at Lake George. Somehow, the sand is softer, cleaner, and more inviting than most locations. Although Barbara and I tried to get there occasionally with the girls, a trip there with Spike and Frank and their families was certainly special. Despite the fact that we could blame our busy lives for not getting together more often, that simply was not a good reason for not doing so. I suppose that's one reason why this visit together was so special. The beach was only our first step in our get-together at Lake George.

Let's face it. Even though we were long-time friends, when I think about it, we were also intense competitors. Who could think up the craziest pranks? Who could throw the hardest and the fastest? Who could score the most points? Who would get the girl? Who would have the most fruitful career? So, it was not surprising when Frank looked out on the beach, saw a parasailer, and said "I'm going up." I said, "Yeah, let's do it."

"Sure," Spike said, "you've had parachute jumping experience in the Army and you and Laura did it from an airplane for fun. Of course, you want to go up."

"That doesn't look anywhere near as tough – or dangerous – as jumping out of an airplane," I said.

"Still," Spike said, "I don't think it's a walk in the park. Maybe I'll think about this."

"Tell you what," Frank said, "no pressure. I'll just go up there for kicks and for the kids to enjoy the courage of their father, then if anybody wants to replicate my activity, so be it."

"What a showboat," I said.

"First I watch you," Spike said, "then I'll think it over."

A man of action, Frank left us and proceeded to the section of the beach reserved for parasailing takeoffs and landings. The rest of us watched in awe with no little amount of anxiety. This is how it worked. An extremely long towline was attached to a motor boat and to a parachair with a passenger strapped inside the chair. The flyer runs along the beach a few steps with the help of assistants. Simultaneously, the boat speeds off deep into the lake. Up into the skies goes the rider for as expansive view of the lake and the immense area surrounding the lake. After the boat speeds in a wide circle within the lake, magically the boat slows and delivers the rider in the chute to a soft landing back in the area of the beach that was the takeoff point.

Frank's trip went exactly as advertised. I truly doubt that Frank's heart skipped a single beat. Casually, it seems, he rode to the heights provided by the extravaganza and, ten minutes later, floated to a flawless landing. I went next, with some apprehension, while Spike was "still thinking about it."

Not only did my heart skip a beat as I was lifted into the air by the two assistants, but my brain took a few spins. From there on, however, it was pure aesthetic beauty. The sky opened up to me as though the soft, white clouds were reaching down to beckon me to them. As I floated upward, my vision became even more expansive, providing a view of the skies, the ground, and the lake in one vast Technicolor photo. I marveled at the way I could take in so much with so little effort. All 190 pounds of me were seemingly light as the proverbial feather. Peter Pan did not fly with such ease.

The ride was too quickly over as the speedboat made its turn and headed back toward the beach. I descended with all of the aplomb of a superhero to the resounding applause of my family and my friends' families.

Only then, I think, did Spike become enthusiastic. Not that many years ago, as Governor, Spike would have been surrounded by security, political friends, and the press if he had engaged in this circus activity. But when it was just us, the former Governor took his turn at parasailing. He, too, rose from the beach flawlessly, lifting into the now setting sun. On the beach, we cheered to see him go so high, apparently enjoying the flight. Then, however, the script changed. After completing the circle in the sky, the chute suddenly overshot the landing area upon descent. Much to our amazement, he didn't alight in the designated area on the beach. Instead, he stayed afloat for a few hundred more feet and crashed unceremoniously into a fragile wooden fence surrounding one of the many large homes directly north of the beach area.

Our entire group, led by Frank and me, sprinted to the spot where Spike smashed through the fence. When we arrived there, we saw a fence bowled over with Spike on the other side.

"How was that landing?" he said, laughing – just sitting there on the ground laughing.

"You're okay, Spike?" I asked.

"More than one of my political foes accused me of being on the fence," he joked. "This time they're right."

"It could have been worse," Frank said. "It could have been me crashing through the fence."

"Or, worse than that," I said, "me."

While all of this was going on, we noted the various reactions of the children we had brought to this reunion of old friends. Frank's David, now 15, and Mark, 13, were not impressed. They had seen not only their father but their mother jump out of an airplane. They were aware of their father's Army career and were reminded of those times in his life when he continued to talk that Army lingo. Frank was Army all the way even though injuries had required him to leave his beloved Army. My daughters, Mary Lynn and Cassie, were more impressed with David and Mark than with anything else going on, and Spike's son, Danny, was enjoying the beach and getting to know everyone, while Jane seemed to be totally unconcerned.

That's when David made an easily predicted suggestion: "How about I take Mary Lynn, Cassie, Mark, and Danny on an exploration of Lake George without the old folks?" he said. We "old folks" agreed to maybe we were having all the fun and just maybe we should let the kids enjoy the territory without us. When they returned some hours later, I asked "How did it go?"

"Oh, it was kind of fun," he answered. "You know, pretty much what you would expect."

It wasn't until much later that we heard the whole story. That's next.

DAVID AT 17

First, we played putt-putt, miniature golf. We all enjoyed the game, getting the ball through the windmill, hitting the ball at an angle to get it to the hole, banging the ball so that it would spin and return toward the hole, all the tricks and challenges of the game. But that was quickly over so we had to move on to greater adventures.

There was a small amusement park in the city. We headed for that. It had all the rides you would expect, including a giant Ferris wheel. It was the largest I had ever seen. We headed for that immediately.

"I'm going to pass on that," Mark said.

"What? What's your problem?" I said.

Mary Lynn piped in: "He's a scaredy cat."

"I believe I have a touch of aerophobia," Mark said.

"There's no such word," Mary Lynn said.

"Well, whatever you call it," Mark said. "I'm not big on heights."

So, Mary Lynn, Cassie, Danny, and I left Mark looking at us as we jumped into the rocking seats and up into the air. Around we went. I rocked the chair to give everyone even a bigger thrill. Suddenly, the wheel stopped.

"That happens," I explained to everyone. "New passengers coming aboard."

But the wheel stayed in that position. Then we heard the siren with a great deal of activity on the ground. The wheel was stuck! I'm sure that we would have been just fine, but Cassie made it worse. She unhooked her seat belt and looked over the side to see what was happening below. Suddenly, somehow, she was over the side and clinging on to a spoke below. We were paralyzed with fear. Before any of us could move, we saw Mark climbing from below, spoke after spoke. In what seemed an instant, he had Cassie in his grip and back into the chair. He scrambled in with us.

"Is everybody okay?" he asked.

The wheel began to move.

"I thought that you were afraid of heights," I said.

"I am," he said. "This is the last time I get on one of these things."

TONY AT 64

It happens so often that funerals take place in dreary, cold, rainy weather. That's the way it was that day. The rain was intermittent and slight, so bearable. Spike and I stood in the small crowd surrounding the burial plot. As I looked quickly at those in attendance, I recognized only the members of the family, but there were others of our age, probably friends from the school or perhaps neighbors. Then there was a leap of a few generations back. I guessed that those were students or former students.

According to Laura, Frank was never totally free of the pain that began in the jungles of Vietnam so long ago, but with some medication and a great will to move on with his life, he learned to survive and thrive in his happy family environment.

Of course, an American flag draped the casket. A young soldier stepped forward with his bugle and played taps. I've been to a handful of military funerals. That act always choked me up. It wasn't any different this time. The piece seems to hang suspended in the air; all time stops. I looked at the very brave Laura standing between two hulking sons in their military uniforms. Frank's oldest, David, had already reached the rank of Lt. Colonel. His younger brother, Mark, wore the golden leaf of Major and looked so much like his father there in that Army uniform that Frank wore the day he was discharged. I knew that he and his older brother were great sources of pride for Frank in his final days. During those weeks, Laura told Spike and me about those waning days. He had been told by the doctor that he had spotted new reverberations from his injuries so long ago. That was the first sign. Then, there were aches in his body that were new to him - his arms, his lower back – but he chose to ignore those signals in favor of continuing an active life of exercise (he still threw the basketball at his outdoors hoop) and participation in the American Legion and with Big Brothers. He had just left a Legions meeting, Laura said, when he had to pull over to the curb because of the pressure and pain. He grabbed his cell phone to call not 911 but Laura to tell her what was happening to him. His second call was to 911. When the ambulance arrived, it was too late.

Now, two young soldiers removed the flag from the casket and carefully went through the routine of folding it military style until it was a tightly packed triangle. One of the soldiers walked to Laura and handed the flag to her, again a process that had moved me in the past and moved me this day, only this time the person being commemorated with this action was my friend Frank.

There was a reception, of course, that was attended by everyone who had been at the burial site as well as others who had been at the funeral Mass but were unable to go to the cemetery. As is usually the case in these events, everyone was upbeat. The conversations were about the highlights of a good life; the time for mourning had passed at least temporarily. It was nice to hear neighbors and friends tell about their respect for Frank in his years as an educator and community activist. It was wonderful to hear from his sons who, I swear, were more clones than merely sons. Spike and I went back to our office that day with a great deal of pride in our friend's life with gratitude that we were a small part of that life.

SPIKE AT 72

Sure, I enjoyed staying in the spotlight, more or less, even in my old age. An occasional request to appear as a speaker at a college or for a statewide organization was usually welcomed. My talks were never as entertaining as one delivered by a former professional baseball player, but I did enjoy the opportunity to reflect on some of the lighter moments of my career while commenting seriously on the day's more important issues. Beyond that, my life was enjoying life with Ellen. In the few years before my seventy-second birthday, we traveled a bit albeit not extensively. We were basically stay-at-homes. I really didn't have the lust that many have for travel, and Ellen's health, mostly her concern with her long-time diabetes, prevented us from considering any trip that took us away from her doctors for a prolonged period.

Most of our travel revolved around visiting our two daughters and their families. That meant driving or flying from our Upstate New York home to either Arizona or Florida. The trips to Arizona or Florida usually took place in the colder months, of course.

Perhaps my primary recreation, though, was the grand old game of tennis. About four times a week, I could be seen at the local racquet club playing doubles tennis with men in my age category, sometimes a bit younger. While I loved to win and was very competitive, all of us recognized that the exercise was helpful to keep our bodies and our minds in reasonable shape. We also appreciated the laughs before, during, and while drinking coffee after the game.

Tony, also a tennis player, was often my partner in many of the matches, but I found an entirely new group of friends also. Marty was a bit younger and totally out of shape but, paradoxically, the best player on the court with his ability to hit the ball almost exactly where he desired. Cal was a few years older but still played remarkably well with hit-the-ball-in-the-air sudden returns and a knack of being where the ball was hit. Jimmy was tall and dynamite at the net, often putting the ball away with overhead slams. As a group, we were very, very good on some days and very, very bad on other days, but we always enjoyed playing – especially when we won.

"Tony, you were amazing out there," I said after one match, sitting in the club's lounge sipping free coffee. *But what were you doing on my side of the court all the time?* was what I was thinking.

Marty, who was our opponent with Cal, said, "Poacher!"

Wally and Jimmy, who were playing singles on the court next to us, joined us for coffee.

"Did you guys win?" Wally asked Marty.

"No, the hotshot lawyers beat us but not by much," Marty said.

"Didn't I see you miss the ball by a country mile, Spike? How many times do I have to tell you to keep your eye on the ball?"

"He had at least three strikes, but he still didn't go back to the bench," Cal said.

Bullies, I thought. *Just because my tennis has gone down the sewer. What is it with me lately, anyway?*

That's when it all started. I realized that I was hitting the ball, when I hit it, entirely off balance. Then it became a labor to run on the tennis court and then, worse, to walk anywhere. Besides, I was exhausted all the time. Sure, I was a type 2 diabetic, but so were a great number of people my age, and that had never slowed me down before. Then came the hand and leg cramps. That's when I went to see a doctor.

"It appears to be peripheral neuropathy," he said. "That's not uncommon in diabetics, but it is curious that you seem to be having a worsening case although you have excellent control of your diabetes."

"Any medication for this problem?" I asked.

"Not really. You just need to keep your diabetes under control, but let's have you see a neurologist. He might have some suggestions."

The appointment with the neurologist was a few days off so I was back on the tennis court. I made one effort to go after the ball at a distance, but my feet just got in the way of each other. Down I went. I just banged and scraped up a knee and an elbow, but I suddenly realized that it was my third such fall in only a few months.

After the match, Wally, who played with us this time, said, "You're having some balance problems, aren't you?"

"Yeah," I said. "I don't know what the problem is exactly. I have a doctor who's sure it's diabetic peripheral neuropathy, but he thinks that I should have more tests. He says that my diabetes is in complete control so maybe I should make sure it's not one of the baddies."

"Like what?" Wally asked.

"MS, maybe."

"No," Wally said. "You're too old for MS. That's for younger people."

"Or Lou Gehrig's Disease," I said.

"Naw," he said. "Maybe Mickey Mantle's disease or Babe Ruth's disease."

"No," I said. "I don't drink."

"I think it's just because you're a klutz," Cal said. "You never were any damn good at tennis."

"Thank you, thank you very much," I said.

The neurologist spent an inordinate amount of time with me. There were shocks and pin pricks and a close examination of hands, arms, feet, and legs.

"If you're worrying about MS or Lou Gehrig's disease, stop worrying," Dr. Hamilton said. "Look here. See how your muscles have been unaffected in your hand. If you had either of those problems, we would see it right here."

"Okay, I guess that's good news," I said.

"But what you do have is very bad neuropathy. We do have some medication that might help, certainly with the discomfort you're feeling in your feet and hands, but you might also get some help with your balance problems. We'll have to see about that. And it's cheap. How about that?"

"Anything's worth a try."

"We'll have to start slowly. We'll begin with 300 milligrams and work you up to 900. See me again in ten days."

All right. Some good news – don't have one of the baddies – and some additional good news: some medication might help after all.

Before the next appointment with Dr. Hamilton, I had a speaking event, a fund-raising dinner for Governor Ed Jensen who was seeking reelection to a second term. After dinner, my job was to praise him for ten minutes or so before he spoke. I had no problem doing so. In my opinion, he was an excellent Governor. He not only dealt with the State's problems in a straightforward manner, but he had a knack for doing so without alienating most of the people.

At the dinner, I did my thing closer to eight than ten minutes. These days, I thought, people really don't want to hear from old over-the-hill politicians. I introduced the Governor, of course, even though everyone knew who he was, and then I sat down at the head table next to where the Governor was sitting before he moved to the podium.

Peripherally, I saw something just off-stage behind the curtain that didn't seem right. It was a man who appeared to be assisting with the lights, but he was wearing gloves and was reaching for an object tucked away in a box. It was a gun!

We had security people on site. We had much younger men on site. But I was closest to the Governor. I leaped to bring him to the floor, covering him the best I could.

"Gun!" I shouted.

I heard the gun go off just as I reached the Governor. Then there was this sharp, burning sensation in my lower back. Then, nothing.

TONY AT 73

I was in the audience that fateful evening, expecting to visit with Spike for a while after the speeches. Of course when he bolted from his chair, I was astonished. Sure, maybe a younger man or a man who wasn't suffering from neuropathy might have saved the Governor's life that day, but it was Spike who took action.

I found out later that the shooter had his personal grudge against the Governor because of a controversial bill initiated by the Governor involving the cutting of state worker pensions. He had been a maintenance worker at the capitol and had signed on to assist with stage logistics for the fund-raising dinner. Because he had access to the site to do some logistics preparation the prior day, he was able to conceal a weapon then and avoid the screening that took place the day of the dinner.

He was able to get only one shot off before he was subdued by security officers. Spike saved the Governor's life but consequently lost his own. He was hospitalized for two months after the shooting and underwent several surgeries, but, in the end, we lost him.

I have no idea why I'm still here. My two friends died, both heroically, but now I was left with many wonderful memories of them. I'm not a hero, but I continue to live my life in a way that will honor my friends. I've retired from the practice of law and spend a good deal of time running a not-for-profit organization that I started to assist victims of violence. We provide counseling to the victims and their families at no charge, assist inexperienced prosecutors in following through with charges against the offenders, and address groups throughout the state about getting them involved in preventing violence. I guess I'll do this until I'm no longer able to do so. Barbara is very supportive of my efforts. She answers the phone with calls from violence victims, sets my appointments for me, and doesn't gripe because I'm not home. That's because now I work out of my home until I take a trip somewhere in the state to talk to a victim, a victim's family member, or a prosecutor, or to attend a court proceeding in behalf of the victims.

I often think of Spike and Frank. Many days, I'm not all that busy, so it gives me time to relax and think about my life. Spike, Frank, and I had some great times and a few trying ones, but mostly I think of those experiences of long ago – the day that Spike was hanged and how vengeance was ours, the childish pranks that annoyed or amused our neighbors, Spike's gift of gab even at ten years old, Mr. Foley's boxing ring, my incredible shyness, Frank's ever-flourishing penmanship, and the little snowball that fell from the sky. I wouldn't change a thing.

THE END

Review Requested:

We'd like to know if you enjoyed the book.
Please consider leaving a review on the platform
from which you purchased the book.

Lightning Source UK Ltd.
Milton Keynes UK
UKHW011958301020
372542UK00008B/461/J